Menacing Messages

Nancy dropped the minicassette she had found into Professor Parris's answering machine. It was a perfect fit. She closed the lid and pushed the button marked Play.

For a second there was no sound, not even her own breathing.

"You have one message," the electronic voice finally announced.

The tape whirred forward, then back, then settled into a measured spin. Over scratchy static, Nancy heard a strange, hesitant voice.

"Threatening me was a mistake," the voice rasped. "And now you'll make the final payment."

Nancy Drew
Mystery Stories

Available from Simon & Schuster

NANCY DREW® 165

THE CRIME LAB CASE

CAROLYN KEENE

Aladdin Paperbacks
New York   London   Toronto   Sydney   Singapore

This book is a work of fiction. Any references to historical events, real people, or real locales are used fictitiously. Other names, characters, places, and incidents are the product of the author's imagination, and any resemblance to actual events or locales or persons, living or dead, is entirely coincidental.

First Aladdin Paperbacks edition March 2002

Copyright © 2002 Simon & Schuster, Inc.

ALADDIN PAPERBACKS
An imprint of Simon & Schuster
Children's Publishing Division
1230 Avenue of the Americas
New York, NY 10020

Printed in the United States of America
10 9 8 7 6 5 4 3 2 1

NANCY DREW and NANCY DREW MYSTERY STORIES are registered trademarks of Simon & Schuster, Inc.

ISBN 0-7434-3744-6

LCN 2001096924

Contents

THE CRIME LAB CASE

1

The Leader Falls

Everyone looked up when Nancy Drew walked into the room. "I'm sorry I'm late," she said, hurrying to an empty chair at the large conference table. Her low heels clattered across the hardwood floor. "Hello, everyone."

She took her seat gracefully and smiled at the others around the table. She recognized most of them. They returned her greeting, while two strangers seemed to be sizing her up.

"But just a few minutes late on this lovely Saturday afternoon," Professor Charles Parris said from the head of the table. He glanced at the pendulum clock on the wall. It showed three minutes after four o'clock.

Adjoining the room, which the professor called his

1

study, were his office and a small private bathroom. Nancy knew from previous visits that the office of his administrative assistant was next door. Next to that was his private chemistry laboratory. As a distinguished professor and research scientist at Westmoor University he had been given the office suite his reputation and international acclaim deserved.

"And you're not even the last to arrive, Nancy," Professor Parris added. "Some of you know one another, but while we wait for Connor, let's get the rest caught up."

He stood up and looked around the table. The professor was very tall and had a husky build. Nancy thought he might have been an athlete when he was younger. He was now forty-four, and his wavy brown hair, which needed a trim, was threaded with gray. As he spoke, a few laugh lines bracketed his dark blue eyes.

"What a great group we have here," Professor Parris said. "The Crime Lab campers are going to have a blast. I've met with each of you several times as we've prepared for next week. Now we have our first meeting all together. Let's go around the table and each say a few words, starting with my good friend." Professor Parris sat down and nodded to the man sitting to his left.

"Hi, everyone, I'm Hill Truban. Retired army colonel and former chief of detectives in several major cities around the country, now on special assignment to local law enforcement."

Detective Truban smiled warmly but didn't seem inclined to say more. Nancy judged him to be about Professor Parris's age.

"I have to interrupt the proceedings already," Professor Parris said with a chuckle. "Hill is far too modest. He is a leading forensics specialist, and we're lucky to have him home right now. He spends most of his time serving as a consultant for crime labs around the world. When he's not doing that, he teaches criminal justice administration here at Westmoor."

The professor nodded to the woman sitting next to Nancy. "Now, Lia, let's hear from you," he said.

"Hi, I'm Rosalia Mistino, but everyone calls me Lia. I'm a forensics geologist, which means I study the pebbles, dirt, minerals, and such of a crime scene. I'll be an adviser to the Rocks, one of the camp teams."

Nancy caught the fragrance of an exotic, spicy perfume as the woman gestured with her hands. It was hard to tell her age, but Nancy guessed maybe late thirties. Lia's skin was a dark rosy tan, and her wavy brown hair was pulled back from her pretty face with a red headband.

"Again, such modesty," the professor said. "Lia and I met last night, and she's arranged a field trip for our campers to a protected area of a nearby limestone quarry to collect specimens. It will be a special treat for the lucky members of the Rocks."

Lia turned to Nancy, her black eyes flashing. "Now tell us about yourself."

"My name is Nancy Drew, and I'm an amateur detective from River Heights," Nancy began, "just a few miles from here."

"An amateur, but with a reputation and wealth of experience you all may have heard about," Professor Parris added.

"Thank you," Nancy said. "I've known Professor Parris since he served as an expert witness for my father, who's an attorney. I was really excited when the professor asked me to help. I'll be a special adviser and in charge of the camp counselors." She turned to her left and smiled at her good friend Bess Marvin.

"Hi, everyone," Bess said. "I'm really excited about being here, too. Nancy's my longtime friend, and we've been on a lot of cases together, and it's always been fun, although sometimes a little scary, too, but always fun eventually, because Nancy always figures out what happened. So I'm looking forward to helping my team of campers solve the crime."

Bess's straw blond hair flipped around her face as she talked. "Oh! My name is Bess Marvin," she added. Her blue eyes widened, and her cheeks flushed a pale pink.

"Well, I guess it's my turn," said the next person. "I'm George Fayne. I'll be the counselor for the Rocks, so I'm pretty sure I'll be calling on Lia for advice." George was also one of Nancy's best friends. She was Bess's cousin, but there was no family resemblance. George had brown eyes and dark, curly hair. She was tall and slim and looked like the athlete she was.

"Christy, you're up," the professor said, looking fondly at the young woman next to George.

"Most of you know me," the young woman said.

Nancy had met Christy several times; she was Professor Parris's niece. Christy had told Nancy that her dad was a career soldier, so her family had lived all over the world. Christy had gotten to know her uncle only in the last year, after she joined the science faculty of Westmoor University.

Nancy figured Christy was in her late twenties. She had golden brown hair that brushed her shoulders in waves. Her greenish eyes were framed by long, curled lashes.

"Uncle Charles asked me to be a counselor," Christy said, continuing. "I know it's going to be fun."

"Okay, I'm here. What'd I miss?" A tall, thin man charged into the room with a slam of the door. "We're doing intros, right? Perfect." He turned to a young woman who followed him in. She was carrying a professional-looking camera.

"Just take a few shots," the man instructed the young woman. "We don't have much time."

Nancy guessed he was probably in his early to middle twenties. He had tousled waves of thick red hair, penetrating green eyes, and a ruggedly handsome face.

"Connor!" Professor Parris exclaimed. "What's going on?"

"Photos," the young man answered. "Publicity. Let's get this camp on the map."

"But I've given interviews, and—"

"Pictures are what we need," the young man said. He walked to the head of the table and stood next to the professor's chair. "Pictures in the local paper. Okay, we're ready," he told the photographer.

The woman snapped a few pictures, thanked them, and left.

"You all probably know who I am." The young man continued without sitting down. "I'm Connor Brandon, the assistant director of the camp, as well as Charles's deputy on his research project. Because of that, I won't have much time to deal with the day-to-day administrative issues of the camp. I did agree to be one of the counselors. Studying teeth and bones as they apply to criminal activity is one of my specialties."

Nancy immediately sensed a simmering undercurrent between Christy and Connor. For one thing, he didn't seem to care that he'd interrupted her. She glared at him throughout his whole speech.

"Of course, I'm still not as busy as Charles," Connor said in conclusion. "So I'm available to any of you for consult if you need it." He folded his long form into a chair.

"Well, now that we all know one another," Professor Parris said, "let's get down to business." He passed out a folder and a loose-leaf notebook full of neatly typed pages to each person. Nancy quickly glanced through her set.

"Before you get to that, Charles," Connor broke in. "I'd just like to go over the basics once with all of us in the same room. I want to make sure we all have the same idea of the concept and goals of the camp."

"All right, Connor," Professor Parris said with a sigh. "But make it brief, please."

"Charles created this Crime Lab Camp three years ago," Connor said, "to promote an interest in the physical sciences and to show high school students that science can be fun." He paced beside the table as he talked.

"Crime Lab Camp is Charles's own private endeavor," Connor continued, "although the university kindly donates some lab equipment and the cafeteria for camp lunches every day. We also get donated support and services from the local police department forensics lab"—Connor nodded to Detective

Truban—"and a commercial chemical lab, Lamber-Tek, where Lia is employed." Lia smiled and bowed her head.

"As you know, the counselors and advisers—all of us—volunteer our time and efforts for this worthy community project. As advisers, Hill and Lia will not be on board all the time—just sort of serving on call. They'll explain procedures when campers have field trips to the police lab and to LamberTek. They'll also be available to come to the university lab if one of the counselors needs expert advice."

Connor ran his fingers through his thick red hair. "Camp lasts five days," he said, "and campers commute from their homes. Twenty campers are selected from teacher recommendations and students' essays. We have created a crime, complete with clues and suspects, and—"

"Actually, it's time for Nancy to tell us about the crime scene," Professor Parris said, interrupting Connor. He smiled at Nancy. "After all, she wrote the crime scenario with me."

Connor slowly lowered himself back into his chair and crossed his arms tightly over his chest.

"There's a summary of the camp crime on page one," Nancy said, opening the notebook Professor had passed out. "We'll lay out the crime scene in this room, and the campers will come in Monday to survey the scene. They will also receive a list of suspects." She closed her notebook.

"Each of the four teams will get several universal clues and also a few clues that apply to that team's specialty," she told the group. "The counselors and advisers will help guide each team to a different scientific solution to the crime, depending on its clues." She leaned back in her chair, indicating she was finished speaking.

"Very good," the professor said. "Are there any questions at this point?"

The meeting continued for another hour. Everyone seemed eager to start the camp and was confident that everything would run smoothly. After the others had left, Nancy and the professor sat down for a quick recap of the camp clues.

"You and the counselors are setting the scene tomorrow, is that right?" Professor Parris asked as he brought Nancy a glass of soda from the mini-refrigerator in the corner of his study. She could smell the sharp aroma of his coffee as he poured a cup from the glass pot. He sweetened the coffee liberally with sugar, then joined her at the table.

"Yes, we're all set."

"Good. I think we'll have the best camp ever this year. So many good people working on it."

They looked over the diagram of the camp crime

scene, noting where all the clues would be planted. Nancy noticed that the professor seemed a little tired, although it was only six-thirty in the evening.

"Professor Parris, are you okay?" she asked.

"Mmm," the professor said, moving his head from side to side, as if to wake himself up. "I need another cup of coffee." He walked slowly to the coffeepot, poured himself a second cup, and again stirred in a heaping spoonful of sugar.

When he took his seat again, he slurped a huge gulp. His eyes widened as he drank. Nancy figured that was partly because the coffe was so hot. She watched his face as he put down the cup. It drained of color as she watched.

Alarmed, she jumped up. "Professor, do you feel all right? That coffee's boiling hot. Do you need a glass of water?"

"Yes, that might be a good idea," he replied, his words slow and deliberate. I seem to feel a little lighthead—"

Before Nancy could move, Professor Parris lost consciousness and collapsed in his chair.

2

Is Nancy Next?

"Professor Parris," Nancy cried. "Professor, what's wrong?"

She rushed around the desk to the professor's chair. He was slumped to the side, his chin resting on his chest. His eyelids fluttered and then closed.

Nancy took the professor's wrist in her hand and checked his pulse. Then she double-checked it by pressing her fingers on the carotid artery, on the side of his neck. His heart was beating very slowly.

Quickly she dialed 911 and relayed the information to the dispatcher. An ambulance arrived in minutes.

"What happened?" asked the emergency medical technician. While the EMT talked to Nancy, her partner checked the professor's vital signs of pulse and blood pressure rates. The EMTs worked very quickly and wasted no time.

"I don't know," Nancy said. "We were talking, and he drank some coffee with sugar. Then he began to slur his words, and he just lost consciousness."

The EMTs fitted an oxygen mask over the professor's nose and mouth. Then they strapped him to a gurney.

"I'm taking this with us," the first EMT said, pouring a little coffee into a small glass jar and tightening the lid. "It might be some kind of food poisoning, and the doctors can check this out, just in case."

"Where are you taking him?" Nancy asked as the EMTs wheeled the gurney to the ambulance. "I need to call his niece to tell her what happened."

"To Westmoor Medical Center," the EMT replied. Then she climbed into the back of the vehicle and slammed the door.

As the piercing siren trailed off, Nancy rushed back inside Professor Parris's office and called Christy immediately.

"I'll get right to the hospital," Christy said. "Let's hope it's just the flu or something simple like that. Wait a minute! He told me once that he has trouble sometimes with hypoglycemia—low blood sugar. He said he even fainted from it once."

"Maybe that's what it was," Nancy said. She could hear the worry in Christy's voice and wished she knew what had happened so she could reassure the young woman.

"Have you told anyone else yet?" Christy asked.

"No," Nancy said. "I'm going to call Detective Truban next. He needs to know that your uncle is ill. I'm sure the professor won't be able to participate in the camp orientation tomorrow. After I talk to Detective Truban, I'll meet you at the hospital."

"Good idea," Christy replied. "I'd appreciate it if you locked up the office. Uncle Charles told me he keeps a spare set of keys in the study next to his office. They're in a box on the closet shelf. I'll call you after I talk to the doctors."

After she hung up, Nancy looked around the office for some clue to what had caused Professor Parris to fall ill. She wasn't sure exactly what she was looking for, but she hoped she'd know it when she saw it.

Maybe she'd find some remnants of food the professor had eaten earlier that might have upset his stomach or a bottle of medicine that would indicate a health problem. A quick look around turned up no such clues.

Finally, she retrieved the extra set of keys from the box in the study's closet and returned to Professor Parris's office to contact Detective Truban.

The detective's cheery nature bubbled through the phone when he answered Nancy's call, but his voice took on a tone of concern when he heard the news. "I'll get right to the hospital," he said, and hung up immediately.

Nancy took one last look around the professor's office, then locked up and left the building.

She drove straight to Westmoor Medical Center. At the hospital, Christy met her in the waiting room. She seemed frantic with worry.

"Oh, Nancy, it's awful," Christy told her. "Uncle Charles got really sick, and they pumped his stomach. Now it looks like he's slipping into a coma, and they don't know what's causing it. It's still possible it was low blood sugar. We should know more in a couple of hours."

Christy took Nancy's arm and gave her a concerned look. "They also think it might be some weird rare virus," she said. "They even want you to have some tests, in case it might be contagious."

Nancy felt a rush of anxiety but fought it down. "I'd be glad to," she said.

"I can't believe it," Christy said. "The doctors say his condition is critical. I connected with my uncle for the first time a year ago, and now I may lose him." Nancy heard the genuine distress in the young woman's voice.

"What do you think we should do about the camp?" Christy asked.

Detective Truban, who walked in at that moment,

answered Christy's question. "I definitely think we should continue with all plans," he said. "The camp means a lot to your uncle, and he wouldn't want us to cancel at this point. It's important that we don't let those kids down."

"I suppose you're right, Hill," Christy said. "After all, the camp starts the day after tomorrow. We hardly have time to cancel everything by then. Will you be the director, Nancy? Take over all the administration stuff? I absolutely do not have the time to do anything but be a counselor."

"What about Connor?" Nancy asked. "He's the assistant director. Shouldn't he be the one to take the professor's place?"

"He won't have time either," Christy said. "He's Uncle Charles's deputy on the research project and will have to take over there. If he has a chance to head up a major research study that gives him professional prestige, he's probably not going to want to spend time on a local school camp." Christy gave a helpless shrug.

"I'm Uncle Charles's only family," she said. "I speak for him now, and I say it's you, Nancy. After all, you helped construct the 'crime.'"

"All the preliminary work is done," Detective Truban said. "I'll talk to university officials to see what they say, but I'm sure it'll be fine with them."

"Okay," Nancy replied. "I'll go over the professor's

15

notes and the props for the camp crime scene tomorrow, just in case. Christy, if you can't make it tomorrow evening to help set up the crime scene, I'll understand."

"I'll come if I can," Christy said. "I'll call you there tomorrow afternoon with an update. Uncle Charles has a private phone line in his study, so I can bypass the university's voice mail system. I helped him pack up some of the clues. They're in the office in a cardboard box marked Camp Clues. And feel free to use the office next door if you want to. It's empty. His secretary retired last month, and he hasn't replaced her yet. I've been helping him out till he does."

"I appreciate your stepping up, too, Nancy," Detective Truban said. "Charles has a lot of confidence in you, I know. I'm sure he'd be pleased with your decision."

"Thanks, Detective," Nancy said. "Let's hope this illness is temporary and that Professor Parris pulls out of it and can run the camp himself."

"Here's my card," Detective Truban said. "Feel free to phone me anytime you need me. And please call me Hill—everyone does."

Nancy left Christy and Detective Truban and went to find the doctor to arrange her tests. She had to wait awhile, but a lab technician finally filled a vial with Nancy's blood and swabbed the inside of her mouth. Nancy asked a few questions about

Professor Parris's condition, but the nurse revealed nothing.

By the time Nancy got home to River Heights, she was tired and hungry. She realized she had missed dinner.

It was so quiet in the house. She wasn't usually alone, but her father, Carson Drew, was out of town for a few days, consulting on a legal case in Chicago. Before he'd left, he'd given Hannah Gruen, the Drews' live-in housekeeper, a few days off for a mini-vacation. Hannah had been with them since Nancy's mother died, when Nancy was three.

Because of what had happened that evening, Nancy would have welcomed the wise counsel of her father or the warm nurturing of Hannah. Instead she settled for the comfort of a sandwich and a glass of chocolate milk. When she finished eating, she put the dishes in the dishwasher and went to her bedroom.

She peeled the bandage and cotton ball from the inside of her elbow, where the technician had drawn her blood. Then she washed up and pulled on plaid pajama shorts and a T-shirt.

In bed she looked over the materials for the camp. I don't mind taking over the administration of the camp, she thought. It really is pretty simple from here on. And I'm sure Christy and Hill will help if I need it.

"But I'd much rather have Professor Parris throw off whatever made him sick," she mumbled aloud. She did a quick mental body scan and felt sure she had no symptoms of food poisoning or a possible virus.

She pushed the papers aside and snuggled down under the covers. Slowly she felt the blur of a sleepy haze. Then a muffled ringing jangled through her brain. When she pushed off the covers, the sound was louder. Forcing herself back to consciousness, she answered the phone.

"Nancy! It's Christy," a frantic voice cried in Nancy's ear. "I just got word from the hospital. Uncle Charles was poisoned!"

3

The Death Angel

"Poisoned!" Nancy repeated.

"Oh, Nancy, it's horrible," Christy said. "The doctors just called me. Uncle Charles has something called amanitin in his blood. It's a terrible poison that comes from certain mushrooms. There's a whole family of amanita mushrooms, and the doctors are trying to pinpoint which one. Some are worse than others, but there's no real antidote for any of them."

"Mushrooms!" Nancy exclaimed. "Is he a mushroom hunter? Could he have gotten a poisonous one by mistake?"

"I don't know," Christy answered. She sounded frantic. "It's possible, I guess. I just don't know. One of the first symptoms is hypoglycemia. That's what threw the doctors off at first. I'll keep you posted. I have to call Hill to tell him. He knows more about Uncle Charles than I do."

"Is there anything the doctors can do at all?" Nancy asked.

"They're trying some atropine," Christy answered. "Sometimes that helps. And there are a few experimental treatments they might try. I'd better call Hill. I'll keep you posted."

As soon as she hung up the phone, Nancy went to the Drew bookshelves and found a reference book on mushrooms. The *Amanita* genus was indeed deadly. She read: "They grow all over the United States and may be found in several different colors. Reaction time may be from a half hour to forty-eight hours, depending on amanita type and how much a person eats."

A tingle fluttered across Nancy's shoulders as she read the last line aloud: "'The amanita mushroom is often called the Death Angel.'"

Nancy knew she had not eaten or drunk anything that the professor had. She crawled back under the covers and fell asleep almost immediately. The mushroom book lay open at the picture of the Death Angel.

Sunday morning Nancy slept in, not waking up until nine o'clock. After a quick shower she pulled on jeans and a blue sweater that matched her eyes. She went into the kitchen and bolted down a breakfast of cold cereal and milk.

As she rinsed her bowl, she heard a car pull into the driveway. Then a familiar knock announced the arrival of her boyfriend, Ned Nickerson.

"It's open," Nancy called out.

Ned walked through the kitchen door. He leaned over to give Nancy a kiss. Then he straightened up.

"Hmm," he said, his nose twitching. "How come I don't smell Hannah's famous Sunday morning cinnamon rolls?" he asked.

"So that's why you stopped by," Nancy said, snapping the dish towel at him. "Dad's out of town for a few days, so he gave Hannah some time off."

"What's new?" Ned asked, pouring himself a glass of juice.

"Lots," Nancy said, grabbing her backpack and her keys. "Come on, I'll tell you on the way."

Nancy headed her blue Mustang toward Westmoor University. As she drove, she told Ned about the Crime Lab Camp and Professor Parris's collapse from a poisonous mushroom. By the time she finished telling her story, they had arrived at the professor's office. She parked the car, and the two walked into the building.

Nancy unlocked the door to the office and flipped on the light. She walked across the room and opened the door to the adjoining study. Sun streaked in through the open blinds at the window.

"Hey," Ned said, his eyes wide as he glanced around the large office, "these are pretty fancy digs for a college professor."

"Professor Parris has earned it," Nancy said. "Dad tells me he's got an incredible reputation as an expert on DNA forensics. Criminal justice organizations from around the world call on him for help with their cases. Westmoor is probably thrilled to have him on its faculty and doing his research project here."

Nancy noticed that no one had been in to clean up the office. The professor's cup was still on his desk, where the EMT had put it after pouring the coffee specimen.

Nancy walked into the study, with Ned close behind. "We're setting this room up as the camp crime scene," she said.

She unpacked the box of crime clues for the campers. "I want to double-check all these things against my master list," she told Ned, "to make sure everything's ready."

"Cool!" Ned exclaimed as he picked up a few of the clues. "Somebody's tooth," he said, holding the molar up to the light. "And it still has its root."

"Right," Nancy said, spreading out a few pieces of paper. "The campers will learn that usually means the tooth wasn't broken off."

"So it probably didn't come out because of a fall, right?" Ned guessed. "It was probably knocked out by a hard punch."

"Or pulled," Nancy told him with a mock shudder.

"Here's some hair," Ned said, picking up a wavy sample. "Is this real blood?" he asked, looking at a couple of small containers of a dark liquid.

"Yes," Nancy answered. "But for safety reasons, we use animal blood. One of the clues in the camp crime scene is a small throw rug. It has two stains on it. One stain is chicken blood, and the other is beef blood. The campers get samples from the two stains. They also get a vial of the chicken blood, which is supposed to be from one of the suspects. The point is just to match the blood; they have to match the blood from the vial to one of the stains."

"Here are some pebbles," Ned said as he held up a plastic bag, "a daily journal, scraps of cloth, and paper." He looked over the table. "Lots of stuff that the campers can work with. Looks like fun."

Nancy checked off the items as she worked her way down the list. "Hmm, that's weird," she said, gazing at the items spread out on the large wood table.

"What's the matter?" Ned asked.

"I seem to have more stuff than I need," she answered, going back over the list. "This minicassette isn't on the list. I'm also supposed to have two handwritten notes: One is a page from a journal, and one is a page from an account ledger."

"There are four pieces of paper here," Ned said, picking them up. "The two you talked about and these others. They look like threatening notes."

Nancy examined her list. "They're not on here. And there's no journal on the list either," Nancy said, picking up the leather-bound book. "Just a page torn from one."

Nancy opened the journal and then looked at the torn journal page on the table. "The paper doesn't match," she said, showing the book to Ned. "The journal has lined pages, and the torn-out page clue doesn't. But the handwriting is the same."

She looked through the journal. There were many entries. She recognized the professor's orderly, precise handwriting. A funny feeling came over her as she realized she might be reading his private thoughts. She shut the book with a snap and read the threatening notes that Ned handed her.

"'The money by midnight, or it's all over,'" she read aloud from one. "'Meet me at the lab in one hour or else,'" she quoted from the other one.

Nancy felt an eerie chill as she glanced around the room. The sun had risen so high it no longer bathed the room in a bright glow. Now the atmosphere was darker, colder.

"Ned . . ." she said. Her voice sounded strange to

her own ears. It was tight, as if she were trying to close off the terrible thought that she was about to speak.

She picked up the minicassette and walked to the small table next to the wing chair. On the table was the telephone answering machine for Professor Parris's private line. She flipped open the top. The spindles for holding the tape cassette were empty.

Nancy dropped the minicassette into the machine. It was a perfect fit. She closed the lid and pushed the button marked Play.

For a second there was no sound, not even her own breathing.

"You have one message," the electronic voice finally announced. The tape whirred forward, then back, then settled into a measured spin. Over scratchy static, Nancy heard a strange, hesitant voice.

"Threatening me was a mistake," the voice rasped. "And now you'll make the final payment."

4

A Double Crime?

Nancy listened to the answering machine message again. Then she popped out the tape and dropped it in her pocket.

"Was that a man or a woman?" Ned asked. "I couldn't tell."

"I couldn't either," Nancy said. "The voice sounded muffled, as if the caller was trying to disguise it. We need to get the tape to the police, Ned," she continued, "and the notes and journal. If they're authentic, someone was threatening Professor Parris." Nancy felt that chill again.

"And his poisoning last night?" Ned asked.

"Might have been caused by the person who wrote these notes," Nancy replied. She could still hear that scratchy voice in her mind.

Nancy carefully picked up the journal and skimmed it. She scanned the pages, paying special attention to the later entries. Then she took the journal and the two threatening notes to the copy machine near Professor Parris's office. She made copies of the notes and several pages from the journal and put the copies into her backpack.

Finally, she checked the wastebaskets, one next to the minirefrigerator and one in the office next door. She was looking for anything that might offer a clue, but the wastebaskets were empty.

Nancy telephoned Hill Truban at his home and told him she had some information about the case. He suggested she come right over. By the time Nancy and Ned reached the detective's house, it was two-thirty. He offered them something to drink.

"No, thank you," Nancy said. "When you see what we've brought, I think you'll want to check them out right away." She pulled out the items from her backpack.

"Here's the answering machine tape." She handed him the tiny cassette. Then she quoted the message.

"Nancy thinks the caller tried to disguise the voice," Ned added. "We can't tell whether it's a man or a woman."

"Well, I can try to check Charles's incoming phone records," Hill said.

"This is one of the machines that don't give the

dates and times for messages," Nancy commented.

"I didn't think of that," Ned said. "That means that we have no idea whether it's a recent call or not."

"Actually, I would guess that it is recent," Nancy said. "If it were an old call, he'd have put in a new tape so he wouldn't miss any messages. Since the machine was empty, I suspect he popped it out within the last day or so."

"You're right, Nancy," Hill said. "I agree. Voice detection equipment might be able to find out whether it's a man or woman at least."

Nancy picked up the small book bound in reddish brown leather. "I told you that we had found a journal," she said, handing it to Hill. "This is not one of the camp clues."

"Did you look through this?" Hill asked, flipping through the pages.

"Yes, I did," Nancy said. "I needed to determine if it was supposed to be used for the camp and just wasn't on the list. The handwriting is the professor's, so this could be either a camp clue or his personal journal."

Nancy picked up the two pieces of paper with the threatening notes and handed them to Hill.

"Whoa, these are pretty nasty," Hill said, scanning the notes. "I talked to Christy awhile ago, and it doesn't look good for Charles right now. The doctors are struggling to help him because they can't pinpoint the exact source of the poison."

"Christy mentioned the amanita mushroom. I read about it last night," Nancy said.

"It's not just the amanitin in his system. There seems to be something else going on. They're running some more tests. I'm very worried. He's a good friend."

Hill looked at the minicassette. "Now I'm even more worried. Until now we thought he'd been poisoned by accident. I hate to say it, but these items you brought me . . . well, it looks as though he was a victim of foul play. Maybe these notes will give us a clue."

"If someone did this to him, do you have any idea who?" Nancy asked.

"Or why?" Ned added.

"No," Hill replied. "He's had a skirmish or two with people in the past but nothing recently."

"Skirmish?" Nancy repeated. "Like what?"

"Oh, the usual," Hill answered. "Professional jealousy, a student unhappy with a grade. Most of the problems were resolved. Now it looks as if he's been blackmailed. Don't worry," he said in a determined voice. "If this was an intentional poisoning, we'll have some idea soon."

Hill pulled on his jacket and strode toward the door. Nancy and Ned followed him. "I'm going to check out this stuff right away," Hill said. "And let's keep this whole thing quiet for a while. I don't want to panic anyone with the prospect of a mad poisoner running loose."

"Did Christy mention any suspects?" Nancy asked as they walked to their cars.

"Well, she's probably told you that she thinks Connor Brandon is involved somehow," Hill said, "but I don't know."

"The name S. Jackson appears in Professor Parris's journal. Does it mean anything to you?" Nancy asked.

"No, I've never heard Charles mention that name," Hill replied. "Let's hope he comes out of this coma soon, so we can find out what really happened. Meanwhile, Nancy, let's keep in touch," he called out his window as he backed out of the driveway. "You've got a reputation as a first-rate detective. That's why Charles chose you for an adviser. I'd appreciate any ideas you can offer on this case." He raced off before Nancy could answer.

It was a half hour drive to Tiger Jack's, where Nancy and Ned met Bess and George for a very late lunch at three-thirty. Over hamburgers, fries, and sodas, Nancy told the others about Hill's conversation with Christy. Then she and Ned shared what they had discovered in Professor Parris's office.

"So what are you saying?" George asked. "You think the person who was blackmailing the professor had something to do with what happened to him last night?"

"It's possible the professor was poisoned," Nancy said. "Detective Truban is going to launch a quiet investigation. He doesn't want the newspapers to jump on this or the school faculty to become alarmed until we really know what's going on. There are some clues I want to check out, too."

"Like what?" Bess asked.

"I didn't get to read the whole journal, but I skimmed it and copied a few pages." She took them out of her backpack and passed a few to each of her friends.

"Gee, I don't know," George said as she read. "This reads almost as if it were written in some kind of code. I can't tell whether he's talking about real stuff or not."

"Exactly," Nancy said. "Professor Parris wrote it as if he were trying to protect himself—or someone else. Maybe he wanted to make sure no one would figure out the truth in case it fell into the wrong hands."

"Who's S. Jackson?" Bess asked. "That name keeps cropping up on the pages I have." She looked down at the papers. "'Meetings with S. Jackson' or 'with SJ,'" she read. "'Must keep SJ quiet.'"

"That even sounds as if the professor was the one making a threat," George said. "I've got a mention here, too. 'Can't let SJ resurface,'" she read. "What do you suppose that means?"

"That's why I copied those pages," Nancy said, finishing her burger. "Hill Truban said he's never heard the professor mention an S. Jackson. It could be either a man or a woman. I haven't had a chance to ask Christy yet, although Hill knows her uncle better than she does. If he's never heard of S. Jackson, she probably hasn't either."

Nancy took a long sip of her soda. "It looks as if the campers might not be the only ones solving a crime," she said. "We might have our own mystery to unravel. Was Professor Parris being blackmailed? If so, by whom? And did the blackmail have anything to do with his poisoning last night?"

"I don't get something," George said, twirling a french fry around on her plate. "Why were those extra pages and the answering machine minicassette and journal in with the camp crime clues? Who put them there?"

"I've been thinking about that," Nancy answered, "but I haven't figured it out yet."

"You said Christy and the professor packed that box, right?" Ned asked.

"Right," Nancy said with a nod. "I don't think the professor's known for being particularly absent-minded or spacey. But I can't imagine why Christy would drop them in. There are a lot of questions we have to answer. I'd like to track down this S. Jackson."

"I can check the Internet," Bess said. "But I can tell you, there'll probably be thousands of entries."

"Give it a try," Nancy said.

"How about me?" Ned asked. "You guys are going to be tied up partly with the camp duties. I'm free this week, so put me to work."

"Don't worry, I will," Nancy said. "I really like Professor Parris. If someone succeeded in harming him, we're going to find out what happened and how it happened."

"Well, I'm scheduled to work on my mountain bike this afternoon," Ned said. "Give me a call if you need me."

"Okay," Nancy said. "Thanks."

After Nancy made a quick call to Christy, she and her friends paid their checks and then drove Ned to Nancy's, where he'd left his car. From there Nancy, Bess, and George headed back to the professor's office.

"I told Christy to meet us at the office at five," Nancy said. "We're going to be a little early, but that'll give us time to look around once more to make sure I haven't missed anything."

When Nancy parked the car, she noticed the blinds closed in Professor Parris's office. A light shone around the edges of the window, where the blinds didn't quite meet the frame.

Nancy led Bess and George down the hall to the office. She tilted her head toward the door and heard shuffling, rustling noises from the other side. She motioned to the others to be quiet. Cautiously she slipped the key into the lock with her right hand, while her left hand grasped the doorknob. To keep from making noise, she turned the key very slowly. She held her breath, so that not even her exhaled air would make a sound.

When she heard the lock snap, she paused for a moment to see if the noises from the other side of the door would stop. They didn't. Whoever was in Professor Parris's office didn't know Nancy was opening the door.

She turned the knob with the same caution, holding it so tightly and moving it so slowly that her hand started to hurt. At last she felt the latch give, and she inched the door open. She motioned to Bess and George to stay back while she peered through the dark entryway into the lighted office beyond.

Lit from behind, a dark silhouette hunched toward a file cabinet, rummaging through a drawer. Nancy narrowed her eyes to focus on the person's face. But before she could recognize who it was, the person slammed the door shut and glared right at her.

5

Setting the Scene

Nancy felt as though her heart had stopped beating for a moment. She stood frozen in the doorway, her hand still clenched around the doorknob.

"It's you!" Connor Brandon called out from behind Professor Parris's desk. "Nancy Drew, what are you doing here? It's too early for the counselors' meeting. How did you open that door?"

Nancy took a deep breath and unclamped her hand from the doorknob. Then she strode into the office, George and Bess close behind.

"I wanted to organize the clues for the meeting," Nancy said. "I have Professor Parris's extra set of keys. How did you get in here?"

"I'm Charles's research assistant," he answered. "I have full access to these offices."

Nancy looked at the desk. When she had left earlier, it was neat and orderly. Now it was a mess of papers and notebooks. One of the file cabinet doors was hanging open, with papers poking up out of it.

She looked back at Connor and noticed that his face was flushed. Was he embarrassed, she wondered, feeling weird about being caught going through the desk? Or was he angry at being interrupted?

She and Connor stared at each other for a moment, neither speaking. It was like a face-off before a championship sporting event.

"Connor!" Christy's voice boomed from behind Nancy. She stormed past Bess and George to get to her uncle's desk. Then she started gathering papers into neat stacks. "Did you make this mess?" she said. "You know Uncle Charles likes things in order. What are you doing?"

Connor's face got redder. "It's not your concern what I'm doing here." His voice was sharp with anger. "It's between your uncle and me."

Then his face paled, and his voice softened. "How is he? I heard he collapsed. I called the hospital, but they wouldn't tell me anything."

"And they're not going to," Christy said. Nancy could see her shoulder muscles tense under her jacket. "I'm his only family, and anything you hear will come from me."

"So tell me," Connor said. "How is he? What

happened? Was it a heart attack?"

"How did you know Professor Parris was in the hospital?" Nancy interrupted.

"One of the grad assistants was working in the building last night," Connor said. His green eyes narrowed almost into a squint as he answered Nancy. It's as if he doesn't trust me, she thought, as if he's suspicious of me in some way.

"Come on, Christy," Connor said. "What happened? What's going on?"

"Uncle Charles fainted while he was talking to Nancy about the camp," Christy replied. "Probably just a virus." She obviously wasn't going to give Connor any more information.

"Well, how sick is he?" Connor asked. "What about the camp?"

"The camp will continue as planned," Nancy answered. "That's what the professor would—"

"Uncle Charles wants the camp to start without him," Christy interrupted. "He's probably going to be in bed for a day or two."

Nancy wondered if Christy was telling the truth. Had Professor Parris awakened and spoken to her?

"So I run the camp and the research project," Connor said. "Fine, I can handle that."

"Actually, Uncle Charles asked me to tell you that he wants Nancy to take over the administration of the camp," Christy said.

"What?" Connor's face reddened again. "Forget it. I can definitely do both. It's *important* that I do both."

"You didn't even want to be assistant director, Connor," Christy said. "You hate administrative stuff as much as I do."

"Maybe so," Connor said. "But I'm sure a better pick than a meddling outsider." He flashed a quick glare at Nancy. "I don't mind working for the professor, but no way am I going to work for one of the advisers."

"I'm not entirely an outsider," Nancy said with a warm smile. "Also, there's really little left to do from an administrative standpoint," she said. "Just keep the camp running smoothly and maintain the records. I'm happy to jump in to free you up for your grant work."

"This is what Uncle Charles wants," Christy said firmly. "He thinks you'll have your hands full with the research project. Hill doesn't have the time either. Nancy has the time and the detective experience."

For a moment Connor seemed to hesitate, but then his angry expression returned. "I want to talk to him—today!"

"You can't," Christy said quickly. "The doctors aren't allowing visitors for a couple of days at least. Camp starts tomorrow, Connor. Nancy is taking over administration. Period."

"Fine!" Connor exclaimed, slamming a few papers and notebooks into the briefcase that had been lying on the floor. "Then I'm outta here *and* the camp. You can get yourself another counselor for the Chomps."

He slapped a baseball cap on his head and strode out of the room.

"Christy, has your uncle awakened from the coma?" Nancy asked when Connor was gone. "Did he really talk to you about having me take over the administration?"

"No," Christy said matter-of-factly. "But I know that's what he'd want. My uncle thinks you're wonderful, Nancy, and he trusts you completely. Hill talked to Lia and the university, and it's fine with them. You'll do it, won't you?" Christy seated herself in her uncle's chair and stacked the remaining loose papers into neat piles.

"Honestly, that Connor scares me sometimes." She went on without waiting for Nancy's answer. "He's been so weird lately. He acts as if he's got some big secret. I wonder if he's hiding something."

She continued arranging piles of papers across the broad dark wood desktop. "He always seems to be looking over his shoulder as if someone were going to catch him," she said. "If my uncle was poisoned on purpose, Connor's a prime suspect as far as I'm concerned."

Nancy remembered the suspicious look Connor

had given her when she'd questioned him. Could he have something to do with this? she wondered.

"Your uncle was being blackmailed," Nancy said. "Can you think of any reason why? Could Connor have known something about him?"

"Possibly," Christy said impatiently. "I don't know why Connor would hurt him. Maybe he wants Uncle Charles's job. Maybe he wants the research project all to himself, and the money."

"Do you know of anyone else who might have wanted to hurt your uncle?" Nancy asked. "Hill mentioned an unhappy student or maybe someone who was jealous of his career success."

"No," Christy said. "Don't forget, I really just met my uncle. I don't know much about his life at all. He and Dad were stepbrothers. Grandma remarried after Uncle Charles's dad died. Grandpa Parris adopted Uncle Charles. Then Dad was born."

"Do you know what name your grandmother and your uncle Charles had before she married your grandpa Parris?"

"No," Christy said. "I don't think I ever heard it. I'm sure not much help here, am I?"

"Have you ever heard your uncle mention someone named S. Jackson or S.J.?" Nancy asked.

"No," Christy answered quickly. "Why?"

"Might be an acquaintance of your uncle's," Nancy said. "Could you check with your family?"

"Uncle Charles and I are it," Christy said. "My folks are dead, and I don't know of anyone else in my family. Oh, I'm so glad you're on this case! You'll help us get through next week and the camp, won't you?"

"Yes," Nancy said. "I'll be happy to."

Christy looked very relieved. "Thank you so much. As far as I'm concerned, the camp is better off without Connor. Of course now we need a new counselor."

Bess and George looked at each other at the same time and then said in unison: "Ned!"

Nancy phoned Ned and pressed him into service to replace Connor as the fourth team counselor. Ned arrived in a half hour, and the counselors got busy setting up the crime scene.

First, they put a few of the professor's personal items in the closet, out of the way. Then they followed the diagram Nancy and Professor Parris had drawn.

Nancy walked Ned through the details while they all planted the clues according to Nancy's direction. "Remember, Ned, your team will be the Chomps. Not only will you get the journal page, ink, ledger note, lipstick smear, blood sample, and other clues that every team will get, but your team will also receive a tooth."

"Outstanding," Ned said as he watched the crime scene unfold.

Bess put the journal page, ink, and pen on the small writing desk near the window. Christy placed a special throw rug in the middle of the room, under a low table. The rug had been spattered with the beef blood and chicken blood.

Ned dropped the tooth near one of the blood-stains, and Nancy placed a few hairs in an obvious place on the easy chair and near the closet. Christy closed the window on a torn piece of blue fabric. The fabric looked as if it had been ripped from a shirt or blouse by someone entering the room through the window. Bess placed a glass half full of soda on the coffee table. On the rim of the glass was a lipstick smudge.

George sprinkled a few pieces of gravel under the window and elsewhere around the room. The work continued, until finally Nancy crumpled the ledger sheet clue and dropped it into the empty wastebasket.

When they finished, they congratulated themselves with high fives all around. "Okay, guys, that's it," Nancy said. "I think we're ready for tomorrow. Everyone report to the cafeteria at nine o'clock in the morning for the camp orientation breakfast. See you then. Ned, can you give Bess and George a ride home? I have to finish making some notes, and then I'll be out of here, too."

"No problem," Ned said.

As the others filed out, Nancy called Bess back.

"Check out S. Jackson on the Internet," she reminded her friend.

"As soon as I get home," Bess responded. "I'll call to let you know what I find out."

Then Nancy entered her notes about setting up the crime scene and finished filling out some of the administration records. As she worked, she thought she heard a scraping noise, like metal rubbing against metal or stone. It came from the study next door.

"That's odd," she mumbled to herself. She sat still, straining to hear the sound repeated, but there was nothing. Even so, she knew she hadn't imagined the first noise.

She got up quietly and crept to the open study door. The room was dark, but slivers of moonlight shot like sparks between the slats of the blinds. A thump outside the window made Nancy's heart thump nearly as loudly.

She tiptoed to the large reading chair next to the window, being careful not to spoil the crime scene. Leaning over the chair, she peeked around the edge of the blind. A large cat, yellow in the moonlight, trotted across the lawn.

Nancy watched for a minute or two but saw nothing more. Then she let out her breath with a sigh. She turned on the light, but everything in the study was as it had been left earlier.

She turned off the light and left the study, closing the door behind her. Then she gathered up her backpack, turned off the desk lamp, and left the office. She still had a creepy feeling as she locked the office and walked down the hall.

Outdoors the entire landscape was washed in the full moon's shine. As she approached her blue Mustang, Nancy saw a tall form move near the large chestnut tree at the end of the drive.

Her racing pulse urging her to get out of sight, Nancy darted down behind the passenger side of her car. From her hiding spot, she had a perfect view of the old redbrick building. She watched a slender person leave the shadows of the chestnut tree and creep toward Professor Parris's office window.

Her mind jumped ahead to her next move: Get to a campus phone to call security. For a moment she took her eye off the form and looked around. She knew she didn't dare start her car, but she remembered a campus security phone on a pole nearby.

With a crackling of leaves and branches, the yellow cat hurtled from a hedge behind the car. Nancy jumped and clasped her hand over her mouth to keep a loud gasp from escaping across the moonlit drive.

When she looked back toward the window, the figure was gone. As she inched up to get a better look, a sudden sharp pain in the back of her head drove her back down to her knees.

6

Rocks, Locks, Rags, and Chomps

The blow on the back of her head made Nancy's eyes roll. Funny flashes and swirls of light scrambled across her eyelids. For a moment she was afraid she would pass out. She shook her head and took a deep gulp of air to help clear her mind.

"This is what happens to outsiders who butt in where they don't belong," a raspy voice muttered from behind.

It was quiet for a moment. Then Nancy heard the rapid clattering of feet running down the drive.

After a few moments her head felt clearer, and she was able to stand up and take a few halting steps. She was too wobbly to look for the security phone to call in a report.

Instead, careful not to trample any possible clues,

she followed the path the intruder had taken to Professor Parris's window. She stayed alert, constantly scanning the vicinity to make sure her assailant wasn't still nearby.

Nancy saw nothing until she got to the window. Partially buried in the dirt beneath the window was a rusty screwdriver blade, and stuck to the windowsill were several golden brown hairs.

After looking around once more to be certain she was alone, Nancy pulled her penlight from her backpack and aimed its beam at the ground and then at the windowsill.

The screwdriver could have been here for a long time, she thought. But we opened the window when we set up the crime scene. These hairs weren't here then. They must have been left by the person I saw sneaking around just a few minutes ago. Nancy carefully took a few of the hairs, leaving the rest for campus security.

She went inside, phoned campus security, and then returned outside to wait. When an officer arrived, she told him what had happened from her first hearing the noise to being slugged from behind. Then she pointed out the screwdriver blade and hairs on the windowsill. The officer put the screwdriver and the remaining hairs in a plastic bag as possible evidence.

Nancy rubbed the back of her head. It was sore, and she could feel a lump, but she didn't feel dizzy or light-headed anymore and decided not to check in with the hospital.

Nancy said nothing to the officer about the professor or her other suspicions. She remembered Hill's caution about keeping quiet. I'll call Hill when I get home, she thought as she finally started her car and drove off. He can decide what to tell the campus police.

When she got home, she left a message for Hill. She also called George and told her what happened.

"Do you want some company?" George asked. "Are you sure you're okay to be alone? Should you have that bump checked?"

"Really, I'm fine," Nancy answered. "I would definitely get to a hospital if I thought I needed to."

"Okay," George said, "but call if you need me."

"I will, I promise," Nancy told her friend.

"By the way," George said, "Bess looked up S. Jackson on the Internet. There are one thousand, three hundred, and twenty-six Web sites for that name."

"Yikes," Nancy said, before hanging up.

She took a long, soothing shower and sank at last into much-needed sleep. "Need to watch your step," she mumbled to herself as she rolled over in bed. "If the professor *was* attacked, his assailant might be branching out."

At nine o'clock on Monday morning, Nancy and the camp counselors, the professional advisers, and twenty eager campers met for breakfast in the university cafeteria. Before they sat down, Hill Truban pulled Nancy aside for a brief conversation.

"I got your message last night," the detective said, "but it was too late to call back. What's up?"

Nancy briefly told him what had happened the evening before, including the scene with Connor in the professor's office.

"Are you all right?" Hill asked. "How's your head?"

"It hurts only if I press on the bump," Nancy told him. "Otherwise it's fine. By the way, the hospital called before I left this morning. I definitely have no amanitin in my blood."

"Great," Hill said. "I'll check with the officer on call last night to get his report about your intruder." His eyebrows scrunched in a concerned look. "Be careful," he warned. "If the professor *was* poisoned, whoever did it might have changed targets."

For the third time in two days Nancy felt a chill down her back. Hill had just echoed her own caution to herself. "Have you come up with any suspects yet?" she asked.

"No," he replied. "We didn't get far with the answering machine message. All of Charles's recent incoming calls pan out except one from a phone booth downtown. We checked it out but found nothing that would lead us to the caller. I'll keep you posted."

The campers arrived, chattering with anticipation. Two tables were arranged in a V at the end of the long room. Nancy sat at the bottom of the V, where the two tables met. Lia and Hill each sat at one of the top ends of the V. Bess, George, Ned, and Christy were stationed among the campers at the two tables.

Before the breakfast was served, Nancy introduced herself, the two advisers, and the four counselors. Then she addressed the campers while Bess passed out a notebook to each one. Inside were lab safety instructions, pages of text describing lab procedures, and information about each team's forensic specialty.

"Welcome to Crime Lab Camp," Nancy said. "Each of you earned your place at the table, and we all look forward to working with you as you solve the camp crime. From nine until three-thirty, today through Friday, you are forensics scientists." She opened her notebook.

"You'll find a summary of the crime on page one," she said. "I'll just read from there: 'An anonymous caller reports a murder to the police, naming the victim. When detectives arrive on the scene, there is no body, but they do find evidence of a struggle, pages from a journal and an account ledger—written in ink—blood samples, and other clues. There are three suspects: the victim's neighbor, the victim's wife, and the victim's business partner. Or was there a murder at all? Did the so-called victim stage the whole scene to fake his own death?'"

The campers immediately started chattering, already guessing solutions and proposing theories about what happened.

"You've been divided into four teams," Nancy said. The campers turned their attention back to her. She read each camper's name and team and then said, "Bess will be the counselor for the Locks, George for the Rocks, Christy for the Rags, and Ned for the Chomps. Enjoy your breakfast!"

The tables hummed with introductions and enthusiastic chatter all through the meal. After breakfast Hill and Lia left for their own labs. The campers and counselors grouped into their teams, still getting acquainted.

As Nancy gathered her materials, a camper left Bess's team and came over to Nancy. "Miss Drew?" he said. "I'm Antoine Washington." He nodded toward the nametag on his denim shirt. "Someone outside wants to speak with you and Christy."

"Thank you, Antoine. Call me Nancy, please."

The young man returned to his team, and Nancy motioned Christy to join her. When she gave her Antoine's message, Christy rushed to the door. "Maybe it's about Uncle Charles," she said.

But it was Connor Brandon waiting in the hall. "I need to talk to you two," he said.

"Connor—" Christy began. She sounded as though she didn't want to hear anything he had to say.

"Please," Connor said. "Give me a minute."

"Let's see what he wants," Nancy murmured.

With a sigh, Christy joined Nancy as she walked out into the hall where Connor stood.

"Look, I'm sorry," Connor said hurriedly. "I didn't mean to come on so strong yesterday. I need to be involved with the camp in some way. And you're right. I won't have time to take Professor Parris's place as head of the research project if I have to mess around with all the paperwork with the camp."

Nancy smiled at him, but Christy looked unconvinced and didn't respond.

"I can be an adviser for the blood and other liquids testing," Connor told them. "Come on. Give me a chance to make up for brushing you off."

"I think it's a great idea, Connor," Nancy said. "Thanks."

Connor smiled and said he'd keep in touch. Then he walked away down the hall.

"Nancy," Christy whispered loudly while they went back into the cafeteria, "what are you doing? I told you I don't trust him. Why are you letting him get involved?"

"I was thinking of the old saying 'Keep your friends close and your enemies closer,'" Nancy replied. "I'd rather have him where we can watch him. Besides, we're not sure he even *is* an enemy, Christy."

"Okay, you're the detective," Christy said, her shoulders sagging.

Nancy decided not to tell Christy about her own scare the night before. The young woman already seemed pretty much on edge. Nancy didn't want to add to her nervous mood by telling her about the attack on her until she had more information to share.

The shuttle bus driver arrived to take the campers and counselors to Professor Parris's office, so they could survey the "crime scene" in his study. Then they would go down the hall to the professor's laboratory and get right to work. The afternoon activities included a tour of LamberTek, Lia's lab.

The ride was noisy and fun, and Nancy couldn't help feeling sad that the professor was missing it. She caught Christy's eye and gave her a thumbs-up sign. Christy nodded with a sad smile.

The bus finally reached the professor's office. The

campers eagerly followed Nancy and the counselors into the charming old brick building and into the professor's study, where the camp crime scene was set up.

"All right, everyone," Nancy said. "Are we all here?" She looked around. "Where's Bess?"

"She left to check on Mimi Guillaume," one of the campers replied. Her nametag identified her as Janie Silver Cloud. "I saw her walking that way." She pointed down the hall toward the public rest room.

"Okay, everyone look around for a minute," Nancy said. "And keep in mind a popular principle used by criminal investigators around the world. It's called the theory of transfer. This theory states that when someone goes into a room, he leaves something behind and takes something out. Counselors, take charge. I'll round up Bess and Mimi."

As soon as Nancy stepped in the hall, she smelled a sharp odor, like ammonia. "Hmm, the cleaning crew must have been here last night," she said to herself. "That's odd, though. It didn't smell this strong a few minutes ago when we arrived."

Following the smell, Nancy continued down the hall. Something was wrong; she could feel it. She walked faster, past Professor Parris's assistant's office. She slammed open the rest room door. "Bess!" she called. "Mimi! Are you in here?"

The rest room was dark and empty. Quickly Nancy turned the corner, still following the acrid smell.

A crumpled heap halfway down the hall sent waves of adrenaline through her as she raced forward. One of the lab doors was partly open, blocked by Bess's unmoving body.

7

Whose Clues?

"Bess! Bess! Wake up!" Nancy yelled, dragging Bess's body out into the hall.

Behind Bess, she saw the body of another young woman. She pulled her into the hall and closed the laboratory door. The girl was tall, slim, very pretty, and unconscious. Her nametag identified her as Mimi Guillaume.

Nancy opened a window in the hallway of the old brick building. A cool breeze immediately blew through the opening. Both Bess and Mimi rolled their heads from side to side. Their eyelids fluttered as they gasped for air and regained consciousness.

Ned and George rushed up, followed by Christy and the campers.

"Christy, call nine-one-one," Nancy said. "I think

they're okay, but we need to make sure. Come on, everyone—out of the building."

"What happened?" Ned asked, picking up Bess and carrying her down the hall.

One of the campers followed his lead, carrying Mimi out to the fresh air.

"Could be chlorine gas," the camper said after he had put Mimi down.

"That's a good guess," Nancy said, recalling her high school chemistry class. "Thanks for the help, Isaiah," she said, reading his nametag.

"Sure," he said. He had large brown eyes and a full head of dreadlocks. "You can smell the ammonia. We learned about chlorine gas in school. Never mix ammonia and chlorine or you pass out."

For the second time in two days Nancy heard the sound of an ambulance siren approaching the building. A campus security car followed the ambulance up the drive.

"But we're okay, right?" Mimi said, taking a deep breath. "How long were we in there?"

"Not long," Nancy told her. "You have to be exposed for more than an hour for a severe reaction."

"Problem is, it knocks you out right away," Isaiah commented. "So sometimes you can't get away."

Nancy found a few moments to talk to Bess before the EMTs examined her.

"What happened?" Nancy asked her friend.

"I don't know exactly," Bess answered. "When Mimi didn't come back from the rest room, I went to check on her. She was in the lab. I got there just as she fell. I opened the door, and by the time I got to her, I was feeling woozy. I might have passed out for a few seconds. But I fought back and got us both to the door and opened it. I don't remember anything after that."

"You fainted," Nancy said. "You're a real hero, getting both of you to the open door, Bess."

While the EMTs examined Bess, Nancy talked briefly to Mimi. "The door was cracked open," the young camper said. "I looked in through the door window, and I thought I saw someone. I figured it might be one of the other campers sneaking a peek at the lab, so I stepped inside, too. I'd walked only a few feet when I heard a funny noise. There was this strong ammonia smell. I started for the door, but I didn't make it, I guess."

"You're really lucky Bess found you," Nancy said. "The EMT said you'll be fine, but they want to give you a once-over at the medical center. We'll call your parents to let them know."

"Nancy, I just thought of something," Bess called out. The EMTs had popped the gurney up to wheel her away when Nancy reached her. "The lab door was locked," she said in a hushed voice.

"I thought you said you opened the door when

you saw Mimi on the floor," Nancy said.

"I don't mean then," Bess said. "I mean, when I tried to get out. It was locked when I got back to the door. I had to flip the latch to open it."

The EMT pushed Bess's gurney into the ambulance. Then they drove away to the medical center. George rode along with them.

Nancy needed to get the camp back on track. The acrid ammonia odor seemed to be dissipating in the hall, but the lab needed to be aired out. In order to clear out the chlorine gas and find its source, the building had to be evacuated.

Using a gas mask borrowed from the EMTs, Nancy went back into the building and locked the lab. Then she went into the professor's office and telephoned Hill Truban to tell him what had happened. He told her to stay put and he'd be right over.

After phoning Mimi's parents, she called Lia Mistino and told her what had happened.

"Good heavens, that's awful," Lia said.

"I need your help," Nancy said.

"Of course," Lia said. "Anything."

"The campers are scheduled to tour your lab this afternoon."

"They are indeed," Lia said. "At one-thirty. Ah, I see. Would you like to bring them now?" she asked. "I could give them a tour before lunch."

"Perfect," Nancy said.

After finishing her calls, Nancy locked up the professor's office. Outside again, she sent Christy, Ned, and the campers off in the shuttle to LamberTek. Then she waited with the campus security officer for Hill Truban.

Hill and two chemical safety officers arrived quickly. The men wore white hooded jumpsuits and masks that looked like elephant trunks. They carried equipment to measure the amount of chlorine gas in the air.

"What do you think?" Hill asked Nancy. "An accident or not?"

"Not, I'm afraid," Nancy said. "I haven't looked over the lab yet, but I didn't like what Mimi said about seeing someone in there."

"No one's allowed in there unsupervised but Charles, don't you think?" Hill suggested.

"Probably Connor is," Nancy said. "He's the research assistant. He has a key to the office, so he probably has one to the lab. I also want to see how the door latches. Bess said it was unlocked when she went in but locked later when she tried to get out. It might be one of those doors that automatically lock when you close them, but I want to make sure."

Nancy paused for a moment, trying to picture the scene as Bess had described it. "Or she might have been a little panicky when she saw Mimi lying on the floor. She might not remember whether the door was closed then or maybe ajar. Mimi said it was ajar when she got there."

The chemical investigators were out within a half an hour. They told Nancy and Hill that the gas was the toxic combination of ammonia and chlorine that Nancy suspected. They took away a huge jar of clear liquid. There was little gas in the lab by then, so Nancy and Hill were okayed to go in.

They wore masks just in case. Nancy checked the door lock. "It is *not* an autolock door," she said through her mask. "Someone locked it. And whoever it was wouldn't need a key. The person could reach around and flip the lock before pulling the door shut. Bess said she was woozy and might have passed out for a few seconds. She could have missed seeing someone at the door."

"It's not jimmied," Hill said. "Without a key, whoever it was had to come in a window."

"Or through the secretary's office," Nancy said. She walked to the door leading to the office of the professor's administrative assistant. It was unlocked. She walked through the assistant's office to the door leading to the hall. "Look," she said. "It's unlocked, too."

"No way this should be unlocked," Hill said. "Someone definitely came in through here."

"This doesn't look jimmied either," Nancy said.

"But this kind of lock can be picked pretty easily." She blushed as Hill gave her a quizzical look. He seemed to wonder how she knew that.

Nancy and Hill finished checking the lab but found no more clues. Hill took fingerprint samples from the door, but both agreed the culprit would have worn gloves and at least a mask to be able to release the gas. They left, and Hill dropped Nancy off at the medical center.

Nancy found Bess, George, and Mimi in the outpatient ward. Bess and Mimi rested on beds, eating a light lunch of soup, gelatin, and rolls. George was drinking juice and eating an energy bar. Nancy got a can of juice, peanut butter crackers, and an apple from the vending machine and joined them.

After lunch she checked on Professor Parris, but his condition hadn't changed. At one o'clock Hill called Nancy at the hospital. He told her that the chemicals team had reopened the building with Professor Parris's office and lab. Soon after that the hospital released Bess and Mimi.

The shuttle bus picked up the campers, Ned, and Christy at the university cafeteria. Then the driver swung by the hospital for Nancy, Bess, George, and Mimi and took them all to Professor Parris's office and the camp crime scene.

Again the campers stood around the professor's

study. "Remember the theory of transfer I mentioned this morning," Nancy said. "People leave something behind and take something away. Look for what was left behind, things that don't belong here. Later, when you get evidence collected from the victim and suspects, you'll check for things they took *from* this room."

"There are two bloodstains here," Christy told the campers. "Each team will receive samples from those stains and a vial of blood. You'll test if either of the blood samples match."

Christy smiled at the Rags. "My team will look for fabric or threads that might have been left. Then they'll match them against clothing worn by the victim and suspects."

"Hey, Chomps," Ned said, checking his notes. "Look for teeth or bones. They'll help you estimate age, gender, racial group, and stature."

"Okay, Rocks," George said. "I hear you met with Lia this morning. She's a forensic geologist and says people write their itineraries on the bottoms of their cars. So you look for that kind of evidence—something from the earth that was brought into this room."

"Hi, Locks," Bess said. "I'm baaaack. You're going to check out hair. We'll check if the color is natural or dyed. We can also look for similarities in color, texture, and shape between hairs from the crime scene and hairs from the suspects."

"What about DNA?" Mimi asked. "Can we get that from hair?"

"No," Nancy answered. "Not unless it's been yanked out and there are skin cells attached.

"Okay, everyone," Nancy said. "Look around this crime scene to see what you can find."

For the next hour campers searched the study, gathering evidence and placing it on the large table. The counselors answered questions and helped the campers uncover clues. Teams worked together, and Nancy could detect a healthy competitive spirit emerging.

At three-thirty the shuttle bus arrived. "This was a long day," Nancy told the campers. "And a pretty exciting one, especially for Bess and Mimi. The shuttle will take you back to the drop-off point. Tomorrow morning you'll be picked up there at nine o'clock. We'll meet you here, pass out the clues, and you'll get right to work."

"If you don't need me anymore, I'd like to check on Uncle Charles," Christy said.

"Sure," Nancy replied. "And, Bess, please go home," Nancy told her friend. "Get plenty of rest. Ned and George, if you can stay, I'd like to go over tomorrow's schedule. I also want to clean up the lab after so many people tromped through it today to get it ready for to-morrow."

"I'll take Bess home and make sure she's settled,"

George said. "Then I'll come back. It'll probably be an hour at least."

"Great!" Nancy said. "We'll be here."

Christy, Bess, and George joined the campers on the bus and rode off to return to their cars.

Nancy and Ned went into the professor's lab. They spent an hour cleaning up and laying out the supplies and equipment on their list. Nancy told Ned what she and Hill had found in the lab. "I feel as if I'm living in an alternative universe," Nancy said. "As if I'm in a sci-fi movie. We're trying to concentrate on the camp crime, and real-life crimes are happening all around us."

When they returned to the study, the sun no longer shone through the trees and window. A ferocious storm had blown up, and the room was dark. Nancy closed the blinds and turned on the ceiling light. Thunder roared, and rain pounded the window. "We can start checking the crime clues until George gets back," she said.

Nancy pushed items to the side of the table while Ned read them off the list. As she slid the journal pages and tooth aside, she paused. "What's this?" she asked, picking up a small green plastic chip. "Where did this come from?"

"I saw Dee Haze, from the Rags team, pick that up," Ned said. "It was wedged between two of the floorboards."

"Hmm," Nancy said, dropping the chip into her pocket. "And what's this letter? This isn't one of the clues either."

As Nancy reached for the letter, she heard a click. Then the lights went out. She strained to adjust her eyes to the blackness. "Must be the lightning," Ned said. "I wonder where the circuit breaker is. Hey, who's—"

Ned never finished his sentence. In the inky dark Nancy never saw him coming. Ned's full weight slammed into her and knocked her through the study door and into the office.

8

Special Delivery

"Oomph." Nancy felt as if her lungs had exploded when Ned crashed into her. She was jammed through the office door and into the back of the green leather chair across from Professor Parris's desk.

In seconds Ned hurtled through the doorway and slammed into her a second time.

"What . . . is . . . go . . . ing . . . on?" Nancy asked between gasps. She staggered around the chair, holding on to it in the dark. When she got to the front, she plopped down into it. Little by little, she could feel her lungs refilling.

Ned leaned on the chair. "Someone smashed into me," Ned said, breathing hard. "He pushed me into you and then through the door. He caught me completely off guard when the lights went out."

Nancy reached up and pulled the chain on the desk lamp. Light spilled over the desk's surface. "The storm didn't knock out the lights," she said. "Whoever's in the study must have turned them off. That was the click I heard."

She tiptoed to the study door and slowly turned the knob. It was locked on the other side. She pressed her ear against the wooden door. "I can hear somebody—or something—in there," she whispered to Ned.

Nancy went to her backpack, which she had stored in the office closet. She took out her lockpick. Expertly—and silently—she unlocked the study door. Ned stood behind her as she carefully turned the knob and cracked open the door.

A bobbing flashlight beam betrayed the presence of a human intruder in the dark study. Suddenly the light was steady. Then it flashed into Nancy's face. Instinctively she threw up her hand to shield her eyes.

She heard someone lope across the room and open the window. Rain splashed in on the small writing desk, and the wind slapped the clattering blinds until they buzzed like a snare drum.

"Hurry, Ned," Nancy said, racing into the room. Ned followed her to the window. Nancy strained her eyes into the wet darkness, but she saw nothing. Then they wrestled the blinds out of the way and pulled the window closed.

Ned flicked the light switch. Nancy ran to the professor's bathroom and grabbed towels. She gently blotted the small desk and the items on it. Ned swabbed at the hardwood floor. Then they dried themselves off and hung the towels to dry in the bathroom.

Nancy looked around the study and reviewed the camp crime scene. She replaced clues that had been knocked out of place. A check of the list showed that none of the camp clues was missing.

"Wait a minute," Nancy said. "Where's that letter? The one the camper found."

She and Ned looked around, but it was gone. "I didn't have a chance to read it," Nancy said, "or even pick it up. I don't even know if there *was* a letter. All I saw was the envelope."

Nancy closed her eyes and pictured it in her mind. "It had no return address," she murmured, "but it was addressed to the professor." She thought for a moment. "It had an unusual stamp, very colorful. It could have been a commemorative U.S. stamp. Or maybe it was from another country."

She grabbed a notepad from the desk drawer and drew a rough sketch of the stamp. She also wrote in the colors she remembered. "I didn't see any words or numbers," she told Ned. "The postmark covered them up."

She called Hill and reported the break-in. "That envelope has to be important," Nancy told the detective. "Someone wanted it badly enough to break in and steal it."

"I think you're right," Hill said. "I need a copy of your drawing so I can run it through our computer. I have software that will identify it."

"That's cool," Nancy said. "Have you learned anything from any of the clues I've turned over?"

"There were no fingerprints on the screwdriver blade outside the window," Hill said with a sigh. "So if the intruder used it that night, he was wearing gloves."

"Or it could have been there for ages," Nancy added. "It was pretty rusty."

"That's right," Hill said. "I also got no fingerprints from the lab, as we expected."

"Whoever mixed the chlorine gas was smart enough to use gloves, too," Nancy said.

"That's right," Hill replied. "And according to our voice recognition equipment, your hunch was right. The caller on the answering machine tape probably tried to disguise the voice. It'll be difficult to trace. But we might be able to use it for confirmation when we get a suspect."

"We have to figure it's probably someone Professor Parris knew, though," Nancy remarked. "When a caller disguises the voice, it's usually so that it won't be recognized by the person being called. What about the two threatening notes?" Nancy asked.

"Nothing," Hill said. "No prints, nothing distinctive to trace." He thanked Nancy for her help, warned her to be careful, and they hung up.

Nancy walked back into the office. "I want to make sure that envelope has nothing to do with the camp crime, just in case," she told Ned.

"It's not on the list," Ned said.

"I know," Nancy said, "but Professor Parris told me he thought of a lot of clues and rejected some. His master list should be in the file."

Nancy unlocked the file cabinet labeled "C-D." She took out the large, thick file labeled "Crime Lab Camp." As she carefully leafed through it, George walked in with a large pizza and a bag of sodas. The clock on the wall said seven-fifteen.

"Food!" Ned said. "We need this. We've been working hard, getting thrown around, being locked out, and chasing bad guys."

"Excuse me?" George said.

"Well, there's nothing about a letter with a strange colorful stamp and no mention of a small piece of green plastic," Nancy said, putting the Crime Lab Camp master file back into the cabinet.

Between bites of pizza, Nancy and Ned told

George what she'd missed. "Every time we set up the crime scene, more clues appear," George said.

"Or disappear," Nancy said. "I feel as if I'm taking two steps forward and one back. I have to find out how and why the professor was poisoned. I'm going to stop by the hospital in the morning and look around a little. Maybe I can learn more about the actual poisoning."

She looked around the room. She pictured the scene when she had entered the evening before. "Remember when we surprised Connor here last night?" she asked the others.

"Yes," George answered.

Ned's mouth was full of pizza, so he just nodded.

"He was standing at the file cabinets and looking in the top drawer of the middle set," Nancy said, walking over to the wall of files.

She looked at the drawer. It was labeled "J-K-L." She opened the door and fingered through the files until she got to one marked "SJ." She pulled out the folder. It was empty. "I wonder what might have been in this file."

"Come on and finish your pizza," George said. "Maybe the file will turn up."

The three friends reviewed the next day's camp schedule while they finished eating. "Remember, I'm stopping by the hospital in the morning, so I might be a little late getting to camp," Nancy said.

"You two take charge of passing out the clues to the campers. Universal clues first, and then the unique clues for each team."

"After that, I take the Rocks out to the limestone quarry to collect samples," George said. "Lia gave me instructions on that." She took out some pages, stapled together. "She's got some meeting in the morning, but said she'd try to get there later."

"Right," Nancy said, poring over her set of the same pages. "The university is providing a van for the trip. It's only about twenty miles from campus. By the time you get back and get your samples cataloged and sorted, it'll probably be time for lunch. The shuttle will arrive to take everyone to the university cafeteria. I should be here before then."

Nancy locked the office. Ned drove Nancy to her car, and the three took their own cars home.

Nancy spent the rest of the evening writing the daily report of the camp's activities and drawing the mysterious stamp she'd seen on the missing envelope. She used colored pencils and tried to get in whatever details she remembered. Then she copied the drawing onto another sheet of paper. She put one copy in an envelope marked "Hill Truban." She put the other in her backpack.

Early Tuesday morning, Nancy woke with determination. She ate breakfast and dressed in khaki pants and a red shirt. Then she drove to Westmoor University Medical Center.

Professor Parris was isolated as much as possible in the far corner of the intensive care unit on the top floor. There was a No Visitors sign on the door of his room. A police guard sat outside the room, reading the morning paper.

Nancy stopped at the nurses' station and introduced herself to the woman sitting at the desk. She had been to the hospital before but had never talked to this nurse. Nancy said she was a family friend and asked how Professor Parris was doing.

"He can't have any visitors," the nurse said. "His condition is guarded."

Nancy took a chance and dived right into her next question. "Have they determined for sure whether the amanitin came from a mushroom?"

The nurse seemed surprised and a little flustered by the question. "I . . . I can't really discuss the details of his condition with you, Miss Drew, unless you've been cleared by the family, the doctor, and other authorities."

"Nancy, hello." Lia's lyrical voice sang out down the hallway. "Are you checking on Charles?" she asked, joining Nancy at the nurses' station.

Nancy nodded. "I hoped he was doing better."

"I'm afraid not," Lia said in a low voice, steering Nancy by the elbow toward a sunny window in the waiting area. "You heard what happened?"

This was the first time Nancy had talked to anyone but her friends, Christy, and Hill about Professor Parris's condition. She knew she should be cautious about what she revealed.

"Christy told me he ate or drank something that wasn't good," Nancy said to Lia. She didn't really know how much Lia had been told.

"That's right," Lia said. "My laboratory, Lamber-Tek, is devising an antidote for him, some medicine to solve the problem. Ah, here's the doctor now," she said. "I'm meeting with him."

"May I join you?" Nancy asked. "I'd love to hear what he has to say and help if I could."

"As a detective, I'll bet," Lia said. "Are you working on this case? Of course you are. You are a great help to the police, I'm sure." Nancy just smiled.

Lia introduced Nancy to the doctor. He reported that Professor Parris was in critical condition but stable. However, the doctors did not know how long he would stay that way. The poison was affecting his liver, and they needed to find a remedy as soon as possible.

"I read that the amanitin could have come from an amanita mushroom and that there's no known cure," Nancy said. "Is that correct?"

"Yes," the doctor replied. "The experimental medicines and therapies aren't working so far."

They talked a little longer, but there was not much to discuss. The professor's situation was grave.

"We're working very hard," Lia told them. "We'll find the answer."

The doctor left, and Lia turned to Nancy. "This is a terrible thing," she said. "Do you think it might not have been an accident? That someone might have done this to him?"

"Anything's possible," Nancy said.

"Have you run across the name Alexander Kabrov as you pursue the case?" Lia's dark eyebrows rose.

"No," Nancy said. "Who's he?"

"A former associate of Charles's," Lia answered. "They had some patent dispute."

"When was this?" Nancy asked.

"Several years ago," Lia answered. "Alex left the area. But I heard this morning that he's been seen around town. It sure is a coincidence, isn't it? Alex arrives back in town, and Charles suddenly becomes ill. I have to look at Charles's lab reports now, but I'll see you later at camp."

Lia walked toward the nurses' station, and Nancy walked to the bank of elevators far down the hall. As she pressed the button, a man with a curly golden brown beard rushed up. A safari hat with a wide brim shielded his face. He stopped suddenly, and his glance met hers.

At that instant Nancy's pulse seemed to skip a

beat. Then it began drumming loudly. He recognizes me, she thought. She felt as though tiny spider feet were crawling around her neck.

The man looked quickly away. He ducked his head, broke into a run, and disappeared through the door marked Exit.

9

The Curly Clues

With a shudder, Nancy shook off the imaginary crawly bugs and took a deep breath.

"Did you see anyone?" A man wearing a tag that identified him as a hospital security guard ran up. He was out of breath as he questioned Nancy.

"Yes, a man raced by and went down the stairs," Nancy said. "What happened?"

The guard ran to the exit without answering.

Nancy hurried back to the professor's room. There was no one in the hall but the police officer who was the room guard, the nurse at the nurses' station, and Nancy.

The guard was talking on his phone in front of the room door. Nancy heard him request backup to check the parking lot and surrounding area. He then described the bearded man who had rushed by her.

"What happened?" Nancy asked the nurse.

This time the nurse did not clam up. She seemed frightened and eager to tell her story. "I got a telephone call for the police guard," the nurse said, "and he came over here to take it. He could still see the patient's door, but he turned his head just for a moment. Suddenly this strange man appeared from nowhere and headed straight for the patient's door. When the guard saw him, he yelled, and the man ran."

"You're sure the man never got inside the professor's room?" Nancy asked.

"I don't think so," the nurse said. "It all happened so fast. The doctors are in there now. The guard checked the patient's room and said everything looked okay. Then he called hospital security to try to catch the man. I don't know why he couldn't chase him himself."

"I'm sure the guard couldn't leave his post, even to chase a suspicious character. After all, we don't know what the man with the beard had in mind. There might have been two intruders—one to get the guard's attention, the other to break into the patient's room. The guard was right to hold his post and call for assistance."

"You're right, of course," the nurse said. "I wasn't thinking." She sat down and took a deep breath.

When the officer got off the phone, Nancy told him about seeing the bearded man at the elevators. She described him and gave the officer her phone number in case he needed to reach her. The hospital security guard returned and said he'd lost his quarry. He held up a few golden brown curls. "This is all I found," he said.

Nancy wanted to talk to Lia about Alex Kabrov, so she asked the nurse if Lia was still around. The nurse said she hadn't seen her but would give Lia the message to call Nancy if she showed up.

Nancy took the stairway the bearded man had taken. She found nothing but a golden brown curl. It felt waxy and slick—not like real hair. Then she drove to Hill's office. His assistant handed Nancy a note with her name on it.

"Gone to Chicago to check lead," the detective had written. "Will be back later this afternoon." Nancy gave the envelope with the sketch of the colorful stamp to Hill's assistant. Then she drove to the Crime Lab Camp. It was nearly eleven o'clock when she arrived.

"Things are going great," Bess said, greeting Nancy. "We passed out the clues."

She reported that each team had been given a set of the universal clues: the inked pages from a journal and a ledger plus a sample of ink from the bottle on the desk, the vial of chicken blood and a sample of the two types of blood from the rug, a sample of the lipstick smear from the glass and a tube of lipstick from the victim's wife, and fingerprints from the crime scene and from all three suspects and the victim.

"Then we gave the teams their special clues," Bess told Nancy. "The Rocks got gravel, the Locks got hair, the Rags got the scrap of blue cloth, and the Chomps got the tooth."

The teams were working in different corners, partitioned off by screens.

"Christy set up lipstick testing for the teams before joining her Rags in their corner," Bess said. "And Connor's here. He was late, but he's starting them with the ink and blood tests."

"Everything's humming along," Nancy said.

"They were asking about the fingerprints," Bess said. "Detective Truban was supposed to talk to them about that, but he's not here yet. We were hoping you'd get them started when you got here. You know a lot about fingerprints."

"Hill had to go to Chicago," Nancy said, "but I'll be glad to talk about the prints. We've got about forty-five minutes before lunch."

"George told me what happened last night," Bess said. "Can you draw out the stamp you saw? I can check it on the Internet. There are lots of stamp-collecting sites."

Nancy gave her the extra sketch she had brought

in her backpack. Then she told Bess about the incident at the hospital and about Alex Kabrov.

"Wow!" Bess exclaimed. "If he's back in town, he could be a major suspect. Do you think he could have poisoned Professor Parris."

"I'll know more after I talk to Lia again," Nancy said. "I want to talk to the person who told her Kabrov was back in town. I want to know where he was seen and when. Is he here just to visit? Moving back? Or on a more dangerous mission? I left word to have Lia call me. If she doesn't get the message, I'll talk to her here this afternoon. She's checking in with the Rocks when they return from their field trip."

Nancy and Bess gathered the rest of the campers together at the side of the lab. Several chairs were collected there in front of a chalkboard, slide screen, and bank of computer monitors.

"Usually you can't get fingerprints from cloth or leather," she told the campers. "It's also hard to get them from concrete and stucco or other rough-textured surfaces."

Nancy drew a couple of fingerprint samples on the board. "Believe it or not, people first started identifying fingerprints in 1700 B.C. Now we have AFIS, the Automated Fingerprint Identification Systems. AFIS computers cost around a million dollars. Investigators can check a single print against any fingerprints on file."

She turned to the chalkboard. "Two prints, even matching ones, usually don't look alike. Why do you suppose that is?"

"Sometimes bad guys get their fingers altered so the prints change?" Isaiah, the camper who had carried Mimi away from the chlorine gas, offered this possibility.

"Sometimes," Nancy said. "There have been cases where criminals have had the pads of their fingers surgically removed or scarred. But what if they didn't do that? What could cause two prints from the same finger to look different? What is it about skin that could make it change from one moment to the next?"

"It stretches," said Mario Macri, one of Ned's Chomps, opening and closing his hand.

"That's right," Nancy said. "So when we compare fingerprints, we don't settle for a first glance. We look for what the experts call minutia points. There are ninety to one hundred and twenty-five minutia points in an average fingerprint."

Nancy circled some places on the two prints on the chalkboard. "These are places where ridges end or where they divide. A real expert can match two prints with as few as seven matching points."

She smiled at the campers. "Okay, let's get our stations cleaned up. The shuttle will be here shortly to take us to lunch. When we get back, you can pretend you're an expert or you can pretend you're a computer on AFIS. Either way, see what prints you can match."

The Rags and Chomps went to their corners to clean up. Nancy joined Bess and the Locks at their station. "Tell Nancy what you discovered this morning," Bess said to her team proudly.

"The hair we got isn't human," Antoine Washington said.

"It's dog hair," Mimi Guillaume announced. She and Antoine gave each other a high five.

"That's cool," Nancy said. "Now you can study the backgrounds you have of the people involved in the crime—the victim and the suspects—and you can think of a scenario in which dog hairs might end up at the crime scene."

On the bus ride to the cafeteria the conversation was lively. Nancy noticed that the teams were excited about unraveling their clues. They also were careful not to tell the other teams what they'd discovered.

The fun continued through the meal of tacos and burritos. On the ride back counselors and campers grouped in their teams and talked quietly about their strategies for the afternoon.

When they got back to the lab, Nancy pulled

Christy aside. "We need to talk," Nancy said.

"Sure," Christy said. They went into the professor's assistant's office, next to the lab. Nancy shut the door.

"What is it?" Christy asked. "Has something happened with Uncle Charles?"

Nancy told Christy what had happened at the hospital. She assured Christy that everything had seemed to be under control when she had left. Then Nancy asked Christy about Alex Kabrov.

"I've never met him," Christy said. "But I heard Uncle Charles mention him once. It all happened long before I knew my uncle."

"Lia told me that Professor Parris and Kabrov had a patent dispute," Nancy said.

"That's right," Christy replied. "Uncle Charles created a new biometrics procedure. It was a way to map the pattern of blood vessels in someone's eye. Investigators could use the pattern to identify the person."

Christy stared at the corner of the ceiling. She looked as if she were trying to remember the story. "Getting a patent is a long, involved process," she finally said. "While Uncle Charles was going through it, Kabrov filed for a patent for the same procedure. Uncle Charles sued and proved that Alex had stolen his research and idea."

"What happened then?" Nancy asked.

"Kabrov warned Uncle Charles that he would pay for humiliating him and ruining his international reputation," Christy said. A few worry lines creased her forehead.

"But he didn't scare Uncle Charles, of course," she said, "and nothing ever happened. Kabrov eventually left town. Uncle Charles heard he'd actually left the country." Christy's worry lines got deeper. "Why are you asking me all this, Nancy?"

"I don't want to alarm you, but you'll hear this from Lia, I'm sure," Nancy said. "She's heard that Kabrov is back in town."

Christy's face paled, and her eyes opened wide. "Oh, Nancy, maybe *he* poisoned Uncle Charles. Maybe it wasn't Connor after all."

Nancy looked over Christy's shoulder into the lab beyond. Connor's red-haired head bobbed among the Rags as he helped the campers. He seems genuinely interested in helping, she thought. Could he possibly have poisoned the professor?

"Don't worry," Nancy told Christy. "The police are on this case."

"And you, too, right?" Christy said in a hopeful voice as they returned to the lab.

Christy went to join Connor and the Rags team. Nancy rejoined the Locks for her own investigation. Two campers were comparing blood samples under microscopes. The other three were using chemical solutions to compare the ink from the bottle with the ink on the notes.

Away from the others, Nancy and Bess checked the hairs Nancy had found under a microscope and then used a sonograph to analyze the curl that Nancy had found on the hospital stairway. As she suspected, it was of a man-made fiber. "He was wearing a fake beard," she told Bess.

"A cheap one, too," Bess said, holding up the curl, "considering all the shedding it did."

Then they checked the hairs Nancy had found on the windowsill outside Professor Parris's office the night she was knocked down. "Hey, this isn't human hair either," Bess said when the information appeared on the computer monitor. "But it's not man-made either."

"It could be cat hair," Nancy suggested, remembering the cat that had startled her as she spied on the intruder. At last the words appeared on the screen. "'Ruminant,'" Nancy read, "'camel.'"

"Camel!" Bess exclaimed. "What is camel hair doing on Professor Parris's windowsill?"

"Maybe it's from a coat or jacket," Nancy said. She thought of the person she had seen approaching the window that night. "It was so dark," she murmured. "I couldn't really see the clothes."

The phone rang in the lab, and Nancy picked it up.

"Nancy, it's Janie Silver Cloud. I'm calling from a

general store near the quarry. We've got sort of a problem out here."

"What's the matter?" Nancy asked. "Where's George?"

"That's why I'm calling," Janie said. "We don't know where she is. She's disappeared."

10

In the Pits

"George has disappeared?" Nancy repeated into the phone. "When did you see her last?"

"We had finished gathering our specimens and started out of the pit," Janie answered. "But I couldn't find my jacket on the rock where I put it. George told me to go on up and she'd find it. She said to tell everyone to wait for her. But she never came. Isaiah went back down to find her, but she wasn't anywhere."

Nancy could hear the worry in the girl's voice. "Don't go back down into the quarry pit," Nancy said, hoping she sounded calm. "Stay at the store, and we'll be right there."

When she got off the phone, Nancy told Bess what Janie had said.

"I want to go with you," Bess said.

"I know you do." Nancy knew how close the cousins were, and she could see Bess was scared. "But I need you to stay here. When Hill gets here, tell him where I am. Don't tell Christy or Connor. I'm going to take Ned with me. If George has fallen or is stuck somewhere, he and Isaiah will make a pretty strong rescue team."

"Okay," Bess said. "But hurry, okay?"

"I will," Nancy replied. "I hope we'll be back soon. But if we don't make it by three o'clock, you're in charge of closing up. Here are the keys. Get the campers on the shuttle that takes them to their pickup point. And lock up."

Nancy patted her friend on the back and gave her a warm smile. She wanted to be reassuring, but deep down she felt worried, too.

Nancy went to the corner where the Chomps were working. Connor was there, helping the team compare the ink samples. "Hi, gang," Nancy greeted them. "I have to borrow Ned to help me with an errand. Connor, can you supervise the team while Ned's gone? I'd appreciate it."

"Sure," Connor said with a broad smile.

Nancy walked quickly out of the lab and down the hall. "Hey, what's happening?" Ned asked. "I can tell by your face that something's up."

They climbed into Nancy's car. She checked her notebook for the directions and map to the limestone quarry. As she drove, she repeated Janie's message. Then she told Ned about the incident earlier at the hospital.

"I know that guy recognized me," Nancy said. "Who could it be? I couldn't see his face. His beard was false, and his hat covered his hair. His eyes really didn't look familiar."

"Well, he wasn't Connor," Ned said. "I can testify that he was at the lab all morning. Where do you suppose George is?"

"We'll find her," Nancy said. "It shouldn't be a dangerous area; they don't quarry there anymore. The group was at the bottom of the pit, but in a place totally roped off for safety. Lia and the professor set it up with the limestone company."

Nancy finally pulled off the highway onto a country road. After a couple of miles she saw the general store. The campers waved in relief as Nancy pulled her car into the small lot. She parked next to the van that George had driven.

"George hasn't come back up yet," Isaiah said, opening Nancy's door.

"Janie, you saw her last," Nancy said. "You come with us. The rest of you stay here."

Nancy, Ned, and Janie Silver Cloud followed the trail back to the limestone quarry, calling out to

George along the way. They carefully made their way down the path to the bottom of the pit.

"It's weird down here," Ned said. "Like being on another planet."

Nancy looked around. Huge hunks of limestone lay scattered about the quarry floor like giant misshapen bowling pins. Some were haphazardly tumbled together where the cranes had dropped them, accidentally forming tunnels and caves.

Janie led them to the site where the Rocks had gathered their specimens. The ground was covered with gritty silvery green limestone dust, which puffed up around their feet as they walked.

"Here's where I'm sure I left my jacket," Janie said, pointing to a large rock.

Nancy bent down and examined the ground around the rock. "Look at this," she said. A jumble of footprints made a crazy quilt design in the pale dust, but leading away from the jumble were two sets of clearer prints.

Careful not to disturb the prints, Nancy, Ned, and Janie followed the trail to a pyramid-shaped cave formed by large limestone blocks.

Four blocks were balanced on their ends and leaned in against one another, forming four walls. The blocks met at an uneven peak at the top. There were small openings at the corners of the pyramid where the blocks didn't quite fit together. These formed narrow entrances into the dark cave.

Both sets of footprints ended at one of these openings. Nancy motioned to the others to be quiet and stay put. She walked cautiously around the stones until she saw another set of footprints. They pointed away from the stones. She peeked inside one of the openings. A hazy light filtered in through the entrances and from the top, where the stone blocks didn't meet.

She heard no sound from inside. Slipping sideways, she slid through an opening into the room formed by the large stones. It was cool and damp. She held her breath for a moment, straining her ears for the slightest sound. Finally, she heard a raspy noise, as if someone were struggling to clear a throat clogged with limestone dust.

"Hello?" Nancy called. "George? Is that you? George! Where are you?"

"Down here." George's voice was thin and scratchy, but Nancy smiled at the sound.

"Ned," Nancy called, "she's in here." Nancy turned on her penlight. She cast its beam around the inside of the accidental pyramid until it lit on a dark hole in the dusty ground.

She walked toward the hole and flashed the light down into a shallow pit. At the bottom lay George on a bed of sticks and leaves. "I think I'm okay," George said, "but my ankle's swollen. It's probably sprained." She struggled to stand on one foot. Swaying, she leaned against the side of the pit. "I'm a little groggy." The top of her head came nearly to the top of the pit.

"Whoa," Ned said when he saw George. "So, Cleopatra, is this your burial chamber or what?"

"It feels like it," George said. "Get me out of here."

Ned and Nancy helped pull George out of the pit. George's athletic body was a help. She was able to hoist herself up partway, like a diver pulling up to the edge of the pool. Wrapped around her waist was a blue windbreaker. "I found your jacket," she told Janie with a lopsided grin as she limped out of the limestone pyramid.

Nancy and the others helped George maneuver her way up the path. Ned and Isaiah carried her partway. When they got to the top, George told the campers that she'd fallen into the pit. But Nancy knew by her friend's expression that wasn't the whole story.

It was nearly three-thirty, the end of the camp day. Ned drove the van with the Rocks team members back to Westmoor and their drop-off point, where they'd catch their rides home. Nancy drove George straight to the medical center.

"I think I was set up," George said as Nancy drove. "But I'm not sure. I remembered seeing Janie's jacket on that rock. I went back to get it, but it was gone. I walked around, thinking it might have blown away. Then I saw someone about twelve or fifteen yards away, carrying the jacket and walking toward that pile of rock."

"Did you say anything?" Nancy asked.

"Sure," George said, "but he didn't turn around. He had on a protective jumpsuit, so I thought it might have been a stonecutter. I figured he'd found the jacket and was taking it someplace safe until someone claimed it. He went into that pyramid pile, then out the other end, but he wasn't carrying the jacket anymore. So I went in, saw the jacket lying on the ground, went to get it, and stepped right into the pit."

"It's so dark in there," Nancy said, "too dark to see a hole in the ground."

"No," George said. "It was earlier then, and there was plenty of sun streaming in. I didn't see the hole because it was hidden by branches and leaves. I was ambushed, Nancy. I know it. It was a trap, and I fell right into it. I feel pretty stupid, not to mention sore."

"Can you describe the person at all?" Nancy asked. "Are you sure it was a man?"

"No," George said. "I wasn't close enough."

* * *

At the hospital George's ankle was X-rayed. She had a torn ligament but no broken bones. The doctor wrapped her ankle in an elastic bandage and encased it in an air cast.

"You probably want to get home," Nancy said, "but first let's stop by the lab. I'd like to make sure everything's okay there."

"No problem," George said. "In fact I was going to suggest we stop for food. I'm hungry."

By the time they got to the lab it was nearly six o'clock. Bess had left Nancy a note.

"'I'm writing this at four-thirty,'" Nancy read aloud. "'Ned just got here and told me what happened. He's going to help lock up. Call me the *instant* you get this. Hill never came. Lia did but left when I told her the Rocks weren't back yet. She said to call her at LamberTek when they were. Ned called when he got here and told her what happened. She wants to talk to you.'"

Nancy and George double-checked the lab. Then they went to Professor Parris's office. While George called Bess, Nancy went back to the professor's "J-K-L" file drawer. This time she fingered through the "K" folders until she found one labeled "Kabrov."

The folder was full of newspaper stories about the patent suit. Several reported that Kabrov was a book collector. Nancy slipped an article with Kabrov's photo into her backpack.

When George got off the phone, Nancy called Lia at home. "Nancy!" Lia's voice sang through the phone. "I've been calling and calling you. How's George?"

"She's sore," Nancy said. She had decided not to tell anyone but Hill exactly what had happened until she had more information. "But she's fine. How are your antidote tests going? Do you have anything yet that will help Professor Parris?"

"We're very close," Lia said. "I'm extremely optimistic. It shouldn't be long now."

"Good," Nancy said. "By the way, I'd like to talk to the person who saw Alexander Kabrov."

"A colleague at my lab thought she saw him," Lia said. "I'll have her call you. I'll be at camp in the morning to work with the Rocks," she then said. "George might need the day off."

Nancy and George finally left the building and headed back to River Heights.

"Let's stop at the rare book shop first," Nancy said. "We can get a sandwich around the corner." She handed George the article to read.

Nancy parked in front of Papyrus, the rare-book store in downtown River Heights. George stayed in the car. After a quick look up and down the block,

Nancy entered the shop. Inside, the smell of old books and leather filled the air.

"May I help you?" a white-haired woman asked from behind a large desk.

"Have you seen this man recently?" Nancy asked boldly, showing the woman the photo.

"I know Mr. Kabrov well," the woman said.

"Have you seen him lately?" Nancy asked.

"Oh my, yes," the woman answered. "Whenever he gets into town, he comes here first thing."

"Where does he usually stay?" Nancy asked.

"I really don't think I should say," the woman replied. "But I'd be glad to give him a message."

"No, thanks," Nancy said. "By the way, do you have an old edition of *Huckleberry Finn*?" She wanted to get the woman away from her desk.

"I may have sold the copy I had," the woman said. "Let me check." She took a hoop of jangling keys to a case against the wall.

As the woman fussed with the books inside the case, Nancy leaned behind the desk and looked at the bulletin board on the wall. Many notes were old and yellowed. Her heart jumped when she saw a fresh white one. On it was printed "A.K.—Claymore, 302."

Nancy straightened up as the woman returned. "I'm sorry," the woman said. "I must have sold my copy. Would you like to leave your name in case I come across another?"

"No, thanks," Nancy said. "I'll check in another time."

Nancy hurried to her car. "I think he's at the Claymore Hotel," she told George, "room three-oh-two."

Within minutes she was parked in front of the grand old hotel. "I'm going in, too," George said, and awkwardly followed Nancy up the steps.

"Good," Nancy said. "I might need you."

They hadn't even crossed the lobby when Nancy spotted Kabrov in the dining room. A waiter was placing a large plate of food before him.

"It looks as if he'll be busy for a while," Nancy said. "I'm going up to his room. If he heads for the elevators, do anything you can to distract him."

Nancy went upstairs to room 302. Good, she thought. It's a key lock. She listened at the door, but there was no sound. It took only seconds to pick the lock. This'd better be Kabrov's room, she thought as she slipped inside and locked the door behind her.

She hurried to the closet. On the shelf was a sack from Papyrus with "A. Kabrov" written on it. She looked around the closet. A familiar item lay on the floor: a slick golden brown curl.

She knelt to pick it up and saw a crumpled plastic bag in the corner. Inside were the beard and hat worn by the man who had tried to get into the professor's hospital room. Nancy put everything back and stood up. As she reached for the doorknob to leave, she heard a key turn the lock from the other side. Her hand froze in midair. Her throat clenched like a fist.

11

An Enemy Returns

Nancy's hand was just inches away from the door-knob inside Alexander Kabrov's room. She could hear the tumblers fall inside the old lock as someone in the hall turned the key.

Nancy's throat was so tight she could barely squeeze in a breath. *I can't hide in the closet. He'll probably go there first. If not there, the bathroom. Where do I hide?* Thoughts shot rapidly through her mind. *Under the bed,* she decided. *It's the only option.*

As she tiptoed quickly to the bed, a voice out in the hall stopped her.

"Excuse me, could you help me, please?" It was George. Nancy hesitated, straining to hear.

"I'm sorry," a man responded. Nancy guessed it was Kabrov. "I'm in a hurry."

"Please," Nancy heard George say. "This will only take a minute."

"Well, what is it?" The man sounded impatient.

"As you can see," George said, "I'm temporarily handicapped. The elevator seems to be out of order. I don't mind taking the stairs, but they're hard for me to manage. Would you please walk down with me?"

"But I just used the elevator," the man said. "It wasn't out of order."

"I know what you mean," George said. "I came up a little while ago myself, and everything was fine. But it's broken now," George said. "There's a sign on it saying so."

"I don't believe it," the man said. "Show me where this sign is."

"Way to go, George," Nancy whispered to herself, as she heard the footsteps walk away from the door. The elevator's around the corner. I've got time to get out of here.

She heard George and the man walk down the hall to the left, toward the elevator. George's steps were distinguished by a muffled uneven gait.

Nancy waited until she was sure George had led the man out of sight. Then she dashed out of Kabrov's room and raced down the hall to the stairway at the right end of the hall.

Taking the steps two at a time, Nancy arrived quickly in the lobby. She stood near the entrance,

101

her head turned slightly away. If Kabrov suddenly appeared, she didn't want him to recognize her from the hospital. She watched the elevator out of the corner of her eye.

In moments the elevator door opened, and George limped out. Nancy walked out the front door and waited near the car for her friend.

"Cool, huh?" George said, as they got in the Mustang. "I had to do *something*. You weren't back yet, and he was out of that dining room and onto the elevator before I could think of a way to stop him in the lobby."

"What made him leave his table? Do you know?" Nancy asked, pulling away from the curb.

"Not really," George said. "A bellboy went in with a message, and Kabrov came roaring out. It all happened pretty fast." She sank down into the car seat and laid her head on the headrest. "Whew!" she said with a long sigh.

"You were great," Nancy told her. "What happened when you both got to the elevator upstairs?"

"Well, there was no sign saying it was out of order, of course," George said. "I had made the whole thing up, but he didn't seem to realize it. I just said, 'Gee, it must be fixed,' thanked him, and hopped on. He looked pretty mystified as the doors were closing."

Nancy told George what she had found in Kabrov's closet. By that time they had reached George's house. It was nearly nine o'clock.

"I'm going to call Ned and Bess," Nancy said. "Let's have an early breakfast at my house tomorrow morning. I want to brainstorm about Professor Parris's poisoning. We can ride to camp together. That is, if you feel up to it."

"Hey, I'm juiced after tonight," George said. "I'll be there. I'll have Bess pick me up."

When Nancy got home, she was thrilled to see that Hannah was back from her short vacation. It seemed like a good omen, one Nancy felt she needed at this point.

Wednesday morning Nancy woke to the irresistible aroma of Hannah's cinnamon rolls. She showered and dressed in black jeans, white shirt, and dark green blazer and went downstairs to set the table.

Ned arrived at seven-thirty. Bess and George were there a few minutes later. "I have something to report," Bess said as they sat around the table. "I got home pretty early last night, so I did some homework. That stamp you drew, Nancy? I checked it out last night, and several possible matches came up: Canada, the Falklands, and Australia."

She reached for a roll. "So while I was on the Internet," Bess said, grinning, "I went back to the list of over a thousand sites for S. Jackson, just in case."

She handed Nancy a computer printout. "There were no S. Jacksons in the Falklands. Here are the ones from Canada and Australia. Maybe one of them sent the letter. Who knows? At least it was one way of narrowing down the list."

Nancy looked over the list. Only seven names were listed. A few had photographs. "Good job, Bess." She looked from Bess to George. "At least we've got something here."

Nancy and George took turns telling the others about their adventure at Papyrus and the Claymore.

"So do you think it was probably Kabrov who poisoned the professor?" Bess asked.

"If he's still holding a grudge, he sure has a motive," Nancy said. "And he's definitely in town. He makes a better suspect than Connor. Connor's got plenty of opportunity, but I just can't figure a motive for him. Also, let's not forget, the professor was being blackmailed."

"That's right," Bess said. "The notes and the telephone message—I keep forgetting them. The professor must have a secret in his past. We need to figure that out."

"I just wish we could come up with more evidence," Nancy said. "We have only bits and pieces of things. I'm not even sure some of them are really clues."

She took a sip of juice. "There's the envelope that mysteriously appeared. At least Bess got some information on where it might have come from. Then there's the piece of green plastic that was found after someone messed up the camp crime scene."

"The police have that," George said.

"There's the screwdriver blade that was under the window where I saw that person who knocked me down," Nancy told them.

"Which had no fingerprints and may have been there for years," Ned said. "Do you suppose it was Kabrov who slugged you?"

"It could have been," Nancy replied. "He's about the right size."

"There are those camel hairs on the window," Bess said. "Did you see anything in his room that matched those?"

"No," Nancy answered.

"How about the person you saw at the quarry, George," Bess asked. "Could that have been Kabrov?"

"Maybe," George said.

"I don't know," Nancy said. "Did the person at the quarry look at you, I wonder? If so, it couldn't have been Kabrov because he would have recognized you last night."

"Oh, that's true," Bess said.

"How about the guy who slammed us out of the study and into the office?" Ned asked Nancy. "He's the one who stole the envelope. Let's not forget him. My shoulder remembers." He moved his arm in a small circle.

"I hate to say this, but we really shouldn't rule out

Connor entirely," Nancy said. The person who assaulted me used the words 'outsiders who butt in.' When we surprised Connor in the professor's office, he used nearly the same words, calling me a meddling outsider."

"Well, he's being supernice now," Bess said. "Very friendly and a lot of help with the camp. Even Christy mentioned how cooperative and helpful he's being."

"Of course he might be trying to put us off his trail," Ned said.

"We have all these unidentified people," George said. "There's the one in the quarry."

"And the one who stole the letter and escaped through the window," Ned added.

"And the one who attacked Nancy Sunday night." Bess chimed in.

"And the one at the hospital," Nancy concluded, "who we're pretty sure was Kabrov." She thought for a moment. "But were they *all* Kabrov?"

Then Nancy looked down at the paper Bess had given her. "And who's S. Jackson?"

The ringing phone interrupted her thoughts. It was Hill Truban. "We've got a real suspect to go with now," he said to Nancy. "I found out last night that one of Charles's old enemies might be headed to town."

"Alexander Kabrov?" Nancy asked.

"Yep," Hill said. He sounded surprised. "How'd you know?"

"George and I sort of met him last night," Nancy said. She explained that they were ready to leave for camp and had a lot to tell him. "Can you meet us at the lab?"

"I sure can," Hill said. "Sounds as if we'll be swapping stories."

Nancy and her friends helped Hannah clean off the table and then gathered their things for the drive to Westmoor University and Crime Lab Camp. Ned, Bess, and George said goodbye to Hannah. They left through the kitchen door to wait for Nancy in the driveway.

Nancy went out to the garage. She pushed the button on the wall to raise the garage door automatically. Then she walked around the car to the driver's side.

With a squeaky grind the garage door started up. Then it stopped with a scraping jolt and went back down with a thud.

Nancy looked over at the wall where the garage door button was. A shadowy form stood there, dimly silhouetted by the light coming through the door's windows, which barely penetrated to the corner.

"Who's there?" Nancy asked.

12

Contact!

"Who are you?" Nancy said. "What do you want? You're trespassing, and I want you to leave. Now!"

The person stepped from the shadows. Nancy still couldn't see the face clearly. The person's hands were stuffed into the pockets of a trench coat. Nancy knew there could be a weapon in one of those pockets. Her senses went on high alert. She focused all her energy.

"What I want is very simple, Miss Drew," a familiar man's voice said. "I want to know why you are stalking me."

"I'll answer your question, Mr. Kabrov," Nancy answered, "but not closed up in this garage. Open the door immediately."

It was very quiet for a moment. Then Kabrov

reached back and pushed the button. The door began its creaky ascent.

"Hey, what's happening in there?" Bess called from the driveway. "Are you having trouble with your car? We need—" Bess stopped speaking when the door opened high enough to show Kabrov.

"Stay back, guys," Nancy said without taking her eyes off the intruder. "Mr. Kabrov, why don't you show me your hands?"

Kabrov snorted and brought his hands from his pockets, waving them at her. "Do you think I'm armed, Miss Drew?" he said. "You're the stalker here. You're the one asking shopkeepers about me. It is you who are sending your friends to check up on me, to pull me away from my own hotel room." He glanced over Nancy's shoulder. She was sure he was looking at George.

"Why would you do that? I wonder," Kabrov said.

"And you were the man, in a disguise, who tried to enter Professor Parris's hospital room," Nancy countered. "Now, why would *you* do that?"

Kabrov's eyes narrowed when she spoke, and he took a threatening step toward her. But Nancy and her friends stood their ground, and he stepped back. "Stay away from my hotel and from me," he growled. "Or you'll bring a lot of trouble to yourself and your friends."

He hurried along the other side of the car and out

the open door. Waiting for him were Ned, George, and, to Nancy's surprise, two police officers. The officers arrested Kabrov for trespassing, and Nancy agreed to go to the police station to make her statement.

As the officers drove off with Kabrov in the back of the squad car, Nancy turned to the others.

"When the garage door went back down, George peeked in the window," Ned told her. "She told us it was Kabrov, and Bess went inside and called nine-one-one."

"I called Hill Truban, too," Bess said. "He's on his way to meet you at the police station. He wants to question Kabrov himself."

"Okay, you three get to camp," Nancy said. "You're going to be a little late, but not much. Christy can hold down the fort for a little while. Lia will be there, too, to work with the Rocks. I'll go to the station and meet Hill. I'll get to camp as soon as I can."

Ned drove off to Westmoor University with Bess and George. Nancy headed for the police station. By the time she finished giving her statement, Hill had arrived. He and Nancy questioned Kabrov privately, but Kabrov insisted that Nancy was stalking him.

"I suggest you ask Miss Drew what *she* was doing last night," Kabrov said to Hill. "Why was she asking my bookseller questions about my whereabouts? Why was she hanging around my hotel?"

Hill didn't flinch. "We're here to talk about you, Kabrov," he said. Then he turned to Nancy. "Is this the man you saw running away in the hospital?" he asked.

"I'm pretty sure it was," Nancy said. "The man in the hospital was wearing a beard made of artificial curly hair."

"Well, is this the person who assaulted you outside Professor Parris's office?"

"I didn't get a clear look at that person," Nancy answered. "But this man was definitely hiding in my garage this morning and threatened me. My friends are witnesses."

"I was merely warning her to stop harassing me," Kabrov muttered.

"Okay, we're getting nowhere here," Hill said. "Kabrov, I'm holding you for questioning. I'm taking you to Westmoor Medical Center. Let's see if the police guard and hospital security can ID you as the man outside the professor's room."

While a police clerk processed Kabrov's paperwork to release him into Hill's custody, Nancy and Hill talked.

"I'm sorry I can't be more help identifying him," Nancy said. "Remember, the man in the hospital wore a disguise."

"Right," Hill said. "I'll get a search warrant for his hotel room. Maybe we can find something there that will tie him to one of the incidents. I won't be surprised if we find enough to charge him with Charles's blackmail and attempted murder. There's been a lot of history between those two, none of it good. We can certainly hold him for a while just for breaking into your garage this morning."

Nancy was relieved to hear about the search. She knew they would find the disguise, unless Kabrov had gotten rid of it. "Check the room for traces of limestone grit, too," she said. She told Hill about George's experience in the quarry. "It's as if whoever poisoned Professor Parris is now trying to ruin the camp, too."

"Or even worse," Hill said. "Someone has moved from harming the professor to harming you and your friends."

"Was Kabrov the reason you went to Chicago?" Nancy asked.

"Yes," Hill answered. "I had information that he had arrived there and was preparing to come to Westmoor. I went to find out more, but he beat me here."

"Well, if you don't need me anymore right now, I'm going to report to camp. . . . Oh, and Bess got three possible matches for that stamp—Australia, Canada, and the Falklands."

"Great," Hill said. "Now, if only we had the letter! I'll contact you later to let you know what we find out about Kabrov."

As Nancy drove to join her friends at Crime Lab Camp, one idea kept drilling through her mind. It's the blackmail, she thought. Why was the professor being blackmailed? That's the key.

When she got to the lab, the camper teams were busy with their clues. Lia was talking to the Rocks. George sat with her leg propped up on a stool.

"Forensic geology is really cool," Lia told campers. "We can pinpoint where gravel came from. So we can determine where a criminal or a victim came from . . . or where a hidden victim is. With just a trace of pigment we can tell whether a tire rode over white or yellow highway lines."

Lia showed the team how to slice rocks so that they could examine the specimens of gravel they had collected and the gravel from the crime scene. The campers carefully saved the rock dust and grit, brushing it into a pint jar for separate study. They took the sliced sections and examined them under a petrographic microscope, a special instrument for studying rocks.

Lia then showed them how to use an X-ray fluorescence spectrometer to measure the chemical compositions of their specimens. Finally, they used a microprobe to determine the mineral compositions of the rocks.

While the campers worked, Lia and George came over to greet Nancy. Bess, Ned, and Christy soon followed. "George told me you had a visit from Alex Kabrov this morning," Lia said. "He's in jail now, I hope."

"So far," Nancy said. "Hill brought him here from River Heights. He thinks that Kabrov might have been the one who poisoned the professor."

"And behind all the other stuff that's been going on around here, too, I hope," George said, rubbing her ankle.

"It sure makes sense to me," Christy said. "I read some of the articles about Kabrov's trying to rip off my uncle. It was awful."

"I don't know," Nancy said, shaking her head. "A lot's been happening. I'm not sure Kabrov is behind all of it."

Just before the campers broke for lunch, Hill called Nancy. He reported that after the search turned up the fake beard and hat, Kabrov admitted being the man at the hospital. "He says he didn't want to hurt Professor Parris," Hill told Nancy, "but was curious when he heard his old enemy was gravely ill.

"He was in disguise because he knew his visit would seem suspicious. When he was spotted, he knew he should have identified himself, but he was afraid there would be bad publicity. He said he'd had enough of that for a lifetime."

"What about the rest of the trouble?" Nancy asked. "What about clobbering me Sunday night?"

"He swears he had nothing to do with any of the other stuff," Hill said, "but I don't believe him. We're holding him until his lawyer springs him or his alibis check out—whichever comes first. I will tell you this. We found nothing that even hinted at his being the blackmailer."

"How long have you known Professor Parris?" Nancy asked.

"About fifteen years," Hill said. "Long enough to know he doesn't deserve what happened."

"Dad told me he got his Ph.D. from the University of Chicago," Nancy said. "Where is he from originally?"

"He's pretty vague about that," Hill said. "I gather he had a pretty rough childhood. He doesn't like to talk about his folks or where he grew up. Not very pleasant memories, I guess."

Nancy thought it was odd that even a good friend didn't know much about the professor's background. She thanked Hill, and they ended their conversation.

While Christy helped get the campers on the shuttle for their lunch break, Nancy pulled Bess, Ned, and George aside. "We have to find out why the professor was being blackmailed," she said. "I think that's the key to this mystery. Bess, I need you to do some computer research during lunch. We'll bring you something to eat."

"Of course," Bess said.

"You can use the computer in the secretary's office," Nancy said. "I want everything you can find on those seven people with the name S. Jackson who are from Canada or Australia. Also pull background on Professor Parris. He got his doctorate from the University of Chicago, but no one seems to know much about him before then. Get me everything you can. I'm hoping we can connect him to one of those Jacksons.

"Ned—you, George, and Christy go ahead to lunch, but bring something back for Bess and me, please," Nancy said. "I plan to go through Professor Parris's files to see if I can dig up anything at all that he could be blackmailed for. It's a long shot, but it's all we seem to have right now."

Once the shuttle left, Bess got right to work in the office of the professor's administrative assistant. While Nancy watched, Bess connected to the Internet and began her searches.

Nancy went into Professor Parris's office and looked around. Then she walked into his study. "This is his more personal area," she told herself. "Maybe something in here will tell me about his personal life."

A knock at the office door startled Nancy out of the conversation with herself. As she walked from the study to the office, she heard footsteps running down the hall. By the time she reached the office door, she heard a truck pulling out of the parking lot.

A white paper sack labeled "DeHays Pharmacy" sat on the floor outside the door. There was no name on the outside. Nancy cautiously peered into the sack to see a cardboard box. "'Disposable Contacts,'" she read. "'Emerald.'"

"Is that package for me?" Connor Brandon stood in front of her, gazing intently at her with the most beautiful vivid blue eyes.

13

A Clue Down Under

"Connor!" Nancy said, staring into those intensely blue eyes. She clutched the sack.

"That's my package, right?" Connor said. "I had it delivered here, so I could have a pair for this afternoon."

"Umm, I don't know," Nancy said. "She opened the sack again and looked inside. A page from a sticky pad was folded against the side of the disposable eye contacts box. "Yes, 'Connor Brandon,'" she read. She handed over the sack.

"Thanks," he said. "I really like the green ones better than the blue. Oh—I'll be working with the Chomps this afternoon if it's okay with you and Ned."

"Sure," Nancy said. "Great."

Connor went on down the hall to the lab.

Nancy walked back into the study. She was so deep in thought she didn't hear Bess come in.

"Nancy . . . Nancy!" Bess said. "Earth to Nancy. I had to call three times."

"Contacts," Nancy said. "Connor wears tinted contacts."

"You mean those gorgeous green eyes aren't really his?" Bess said.

"Oh, they're his all right," Nancy said. "He just bought a new box of them. His eyes are blue today. I'll bet the piece of green plastic was from one of his contacts."

"The plastic that one of the campers found at the camp crime scene?" Bess asked. "That was after you and Ned were shoved around in there. Do you suppose Connor lost his contact then? Was he the guy who stole the envelope, do you think?"

"That's a pretty big leap, but it's possible," Nancy said. She thought for a moment. "He was wearing the green contacts on Monday morning during camp orientation. When I saw him Tuesday here at the lab, he was wearing glasses."

"So he could have lost his contact the night before when he was wrestling around," Bess said.

"Today he's wearing blue contacts, but he just got a box of new green ones," Nancy said. "Still, that piece of plastic the campers found could have been stuck between the floorboards in the study for months," Nancy said. "Connor has free access to these rooms. Even if it is a piece of one of his contacts, he could have lost it anytime. It doesn't mean he was the one who pushed us out of there and stole the envelope."

Ned, George, and Christy burst in with turkey sandwiches, chips, and sodas for Nancy and Bess. Bess told them about Connor's contacts.

"I knew it," Christy said. "I just don't trust him. Kabrov may be the really bad guy, but Connor's up to something. I just know it."

"I agree with Nancy," George said. "That piece of green plastic doesn't mean anything."

"Well, *we* know that," Nancy said, "but Connor might not. I'm going to try something after I eat. Ned, Connor's going to be working with the Chomps this afternoon. I think I'll join you all. Christy, can you help get the Locks started while Bess eats? She'll be there soon."

"Sure," Christy said.

While the other counselors started the afternoon camp session, Nancy and Bess sat down to eat their sandwiches.

"I've narrowed the S. Jacksons down even further," Bess said between bites. "Here are printouts for a couple of them. One is really interesting. He was a chemist in Australia named Shep Jackson who was accused of murder twenty years ago."

She put the pages that she had printed from the Web site on the little writing desk near the window. "He was never tried for the murder because the case was thrown out for lack of evidence," she said. "I figured, since he was a chemist, that was a pretty good connection."

"Yes," Nancy said. She paced across the wood floor of the study, thinking. "That's just the kind of stuff I'm looking for."

She pulled the chair out from under the small writing desk and sat down on it. "Yikes!" she cried, jumping up. "It's wet! The chair is wet." She swiped her hand across the back of her blazer and jeans. They were barely damp. Then she patted the chair seat. Its soft pad was wet. When she pushed on it, clear drops appeared on the top.

"Did somebody spill something on that chair, do you think?" Bess asked.

"Maybe," Nancy said. "It got soaked when it poured in here night before last. That was when Ned and I got shoved out by that intruder. But we mopped up this whole area. It couldn't still be wet. Unless . . ."

She looked at the desk. It was a very basic design. It had a flat top, with two small, shallow drawers on each side. Across the front was an elaborate carving of flowers and leaves.

Nancy ran her hand under the bottom of the desk. The wood felt very wet. "The top of this desk is dry, but the bottom is still wet," she told Bess. "It must have gotten wet on the inside and has been dripping down on the chair."

"But there's no drawer in the middle," Bess said.

"No drawer that we can see," Nancy said. She crouched down and looked under the desk. A very narrow crack formed a perfect rectangle on the desk bottom. A few drops fell through the crack as she watched.

Nancy ran her fingers around the desk. She opened one of the small drawers on the right and ran her fingers around its inside. Finally, she felt a tiny metal lever. She pushed it, and a small drawer popped out of the carved front of the desk.

"A secret drawer," Bess whispered.

On the bottom of the drawer a leather envelope lay in a shallow film of water. Nancy took out the envelope and wiped it dry. Inside was an old black-and-white photograph, damp around the edges. It showed a woman in a flowered dress. Standing next to her was a young boy, holding her hand. His other hand held up a fish hanging from a line. The little boy wore a wide-brimmed straw hat. Written on the back of the photo was "Sheppie—7."

"Sheppie," Bess read. "Shep. Shep Jackson. Oh,

Nancy, that could be that guy I told you about, the Australian in that murder case." Bess picked up the computer printout she had given Nancy and read it again.

"This could have some connection to that S. Jackson," Nancy said. She wiped off the leather envelope and blotted the inside of the drawer. There was nothing else in it.

"Come on," Nancy said. "I want to show this to Christy to see if she knows anything about it. I also want to talk to Connor about contact lenses." She patted the edges of the photograph dry and put it in a manila envelope that she found in the office. Then she and Bess closed the office and went to the lab.

Christy was working with both her own Rags team and Bess's Locks. George's Rocks were continuing the work with the rock sections that Lia had taught them to do. Connor was telling the Chomps about using teeth and bones in criminal investigations. Bess joined the Locks. Nancy went to the Chomps corner.

"You can use bone and teeth to find out—or at least to estimate—a person's age, gender, race, and stature," Connor was saying. "Sometimes you can tell what diseases a person had. And even though there may not seem to be any blood on a tooth or bone fragment, identifying blood proteins might still be there. They can also be used in investigating. There can also be traces of drugs. You can use chromatography and spectometry to give you a sort of fingerprint of the drug."

When he finished talking, the team went to work examining the tooth. Connor came over to speak to Nancy. "I got them started, so I'm going to leave now," he said. "If you need me tomorrow, I'll be happy to come back."

"I'll let you know," Nancy said, accompanying him out of the lab and down the hall. "I was surprised to see your blue eyes today," she said. "I didn't realize you wore contacts."

"Yeah, they're great," he said, "and the colors are cool."

"Ned and I had an interesting experience Monday night," Nancy said, watching Connor's expression. "We were in the professor's study, and an intruder broke in, attacked us, and locked us out. Whoever it was stole a letter."

Connor's face paled, then flushed red like his hair. "Really?" he said.

"Yes, and we found a chip of green plastic in the study that night that had not been there earlier. Amazing—it was the same color as your contacts." Nancy stopped and stared into Connor's eyes. He stopped, too. He stared back for a minute, then dropped his head.

"Okay, I was in there," he said. "Look, I'm sorry. I didn't want to hurt anyone. I just wanted to protect Charles."

"Protect him from what?" Nancy asked.

"He told me that someone's been blackmailing him. I don't know what it's about, but Charles swore me to secrecy about the blackmail. I can't keep quiet any longer. I knew there was a letter or something that had to do with the blackmail in his office or study."

Connor shook his head. "I kind of panicked. First he's poisoned, so there are detectives crawling all around. Then Christy puts you in charge of the camp, and you've got free run of his office. And the campers are moving in and out of the crime scene. I was afraid someone would come across this letter. That's what I was looking for when you all caught me going through his office."

"But you didn't find it then," Nancy said.

"No, I came back Monday, found it in a file, and was getting ready to leave when I heard you bringing the campers in to see the crime scene. I went to hide in the closet, but I stumbled. My contact popped out, and I didn't even notice that the letter fell from my pocket, too."

"Then the campers found the letter and a piece of your contact," Nancy said.

"I could hear that from the closet," Connor said. "The rest of my contact is probably wedged in the ridges of a camper's shoe sole. Anyway, after they left, I killed the lights, shoved you and Ned out of the way, got the letter, and beat it out of there. Only there was no letter."

He reached into his briefcase. "Here it is. The envelope was empty, I swear. I'd tell you if there were something in it because I really think it has something to do with the blackmail. Charles is my mentor. He's like a father to me. I'd do anything to help him."

Nancy believed him. She looked at the envelope. The letter was from Australia. "Do you know anything about the professor's background?" she asked. "Has he ever mentioned someone named Shep Jackson to you?"

"No to both questions," he answered. "He got his last degree at the University of Chicago, but he would never talk about anything before that."

"Take this to Hill Truban right away," Nancy said. "Tell him everything you've told me. And have him get in touch with me. I have some information to share with him, too."

Connor left, and Nancy went back to the lab. She waited until all the Rags were busy at their microscopes and Christy had a free moment.

"I want to show you something," Nancy told Christy. They went into the administrative assistant's office next to the lab. Nancy pulled the photograph from the envelope and showed it to Christy.

"Wow!" Christy said. "Where'd you find that old photo?"

"Do you recognize these people?" Nancy asked.

"Sure," Christy said, grinning. "That's Grandma . . . and Uncle Charles."

14

The Brush-off

"Uncle Charles!" Nancy exclaimed. "This is your uncle in this photo?" She looked down at the little boy holding up the fish.

"Yes," Christy said. "And my grandmother, his mother."

Nancy turned over the photograph and showed Christy the writing on the back: "Sheppie—7."

"Yes, that looks about right, don't you think? He'd be about seven years old in that picture. That's probably about the time Grandma and Grandpa Parris got married. I think I heard once that he was just starting school then."

"But what about the name Sheppie?" Nancy asked.

"Some kind of nickname, I guess," Christy said. "I've never heard it before."

Nancy showed her the printout Bess had made on Shep Jackson. "Do you remember hearing that your grandmother's name was Jackson before she met your grandpa Parris?"

"No, I don't," Christy said, her face white. "Nancy, are you saying that Uncle Charles is Shep Jackson? A murderer?"

"It's just a hunch," Nancy said. "We have to find out more about this Shep Jackson—what happened to him after the case was thrown out. It certainly would be something that a blackmailer could jump on."

"But Uncle Charles—a murderer. I can't believe it," Christy said.

"Don't forget," Nancy told her, "the case was thrown out because there wasn't enough evidence, so he could be innocent. But even if the case were never really proved, it would still be something he wouldn't want known."

Christy was trembling, and Nancy put her hand gently on the young woman's arm. "Don't worry," she said. "We're going to find the truth. If we figure out why he was blackmailed, we may be able to find the culprit. If we find the culprit, we probably have the poisoner. Then we can find the poison and help your uncle get well."

Christy took a deep breath and nodded. "Okay," she said. "What do I do next?"

"It's three-fifteen. You, Bess, Ned, and George get the campers on the shuttle and close up the lab. Here are the keys. Then wait for me at Munchies. We can get something to eat and talk over the case. I'm going to track down Hill and tell him what we've found."

Christy went back to the lab, and Nancy went into the office. She called Hill and talked briefly with him. She told him she'd be right over and asked him to check the international files for the criminal record and possible whereabouts of Shep Jackson of Australia.

By the time she got to Hill's office, he had found something. First they talked about Connor, who had reported to Hill as Nancy had advised.

"I believe him," Hill said. "He seems very loyal to Charles."

"I agree," Nancy said with a nod. "Do you still have Kabrov in custody?"

"His lawyer got him out this morning," Hill answered. "We're watching him pretty closely. We couldn't get him to talk, but I have a feeling he's behind the whole thing. It would help if we knew what the actual blackmail was about."

"I may be able to help you there," Nancy said. She showed him the photograph and told him what

Christy had said. Then she gave him the printout on Shep Jackson that Bess had made.

Hill stared at the picture and seemed lost in thought for a moment. Then he scanned the printout quickly. "I got the same information," he said. "And more from the criminal records. There's not much about his early life. He was an American who got his college degree in chemistry in Australia. He was working there after he was graduated when this criminal case came up."

"What was the case exactly?" Nancy said.

"It was some kind of fight or brawl," Hill reported. "Jackson maintained it was self-defense, but the prosecutor kept going for murder. When the case finally got to court, it was thrown out, as it says here."

"But he wasn't exonerated," Nancy said.

"No," Hill answered. "The court didn't say he was innocent. They just said no one could prove he was guilty."

"Then what happened?"

"Apparently he booked passage to the United States shortly after that," Hill said. "But there's nothing more about him. He seems to have disappeared."

"Or come to Westmoor to teach," Nancy said.

"So you're guessing Charles's name was Shep Jackson before his mother married his stepfather," Hill said.

"Well, we know he was called Sheppie from the

131

photo," Nancy said. "We can confirm his last name with a genealogical search to see if his birth father's name was Jackson."

"That'll probably take awhile," Hill said. "Christy said that his stepfather adopted him, so that's when his surname changed to Parris."

"Right, and his name may have been Charles all along and Shep was just a nickname," Nancy said.

"But why did he go back to Shep Jackson when he went to school in Australia?" Hill asked.

"If we're right so far," Nancy replied, "he's probably the only one who can answer that. Maybe he had a falling-out with his stepfather and went back to his original name. Who knows? If we can just find the poisoner and get the full formula for that lethal concoction, perhaps the professor himself can tell us what happened."

"I talked to the doctors again this morning," Hill said. "They think they might have pinpointed another part of the formula, so they're trying something new today. "Lia is sure her lab is going to come up with something."

"Let's hope so," Nancy said. "I'm meeting the counselors now. I'll have Bess start a search on the professor's birth father."

"I have some contacts in Sydney, Australia," Hill said. "I'll get one of them on that, too. Let's keep in close touch."

* * *

By the time Nancy arrived at Munchies, Christy and Bess had shared with Ned and George what they knew about the photo and Shep Jackson. Nancy told them about Connor's confession and Hill's information.

"Oh, Nancy, I think you're right about Uncle Charles's being Shep Jackson," Christy said. "I just wish I knew more about that whole part of my family's history."

"There's something I've been wondering for a long time," George said. "How come those real notes from the blackmailer and the minicassette from the phone answering machine got mixed in with the camp crime clues?"

"That was probably my fault," Christy said. "Uncle Charles and I were planning to go over the camp stuff and pack it together. Then he was asked to do a last-minute presentation in Chicago, filling in for someone else. I thought I'd surprise him and put the clues together myself."

She took a drink of soda. "He works on this camp all year long, trying to figure out the right clues for the campers. All this stuff was in a jumble on his desk. Some of the clues were in the file cabinet. Some were in his desk drawers or in box. I just gathered those other things by mistake and lumped them in with the rest."

"It's a good thing you did," Nancy said. "Otherwise we'd never have known about the blackmail."

"We've got to find out who poisoned Uncle Charles," Christy said, echoing Nancy's thoughts.

"I'm going back to the office tonight to see if there's anything else I could have missed," Nancy said. "Christy, do you have any old family papers, photo albums, anything you could go through? You might find something that wouldn't have meant anything earlier but might now that we think your uncle is Shep Jackson."

"Sure," Christy said. "I'd be happy to."

"Bess, I'd like you to do the genealogical search," Nancy said. "See if you can track down the professor's birth father and verify his name."

"Glad to," Bess said. "Especially if George helps print and collate. Family histories can be pretty complicated."

"I'll do anything that allows me to keep my leg up and rested," George said.

"Ned, you can come back to the office with me if you want," Nancy said. "Two heads are always better than one."

"Can you do me a favor?" George said. "I brought one of Lia's field brushes home by mistake. I'd like to get it locked up in the lab for safekeeping till I see her tomorrow. Will you take it back there?"

Nancy put the brush in her backpack, and they all

went off to their investigations. It was six-thirty by the time Nancy and Ned got back to the professor's office. They first went into the lab, to the corner where the Rocks worked.

Nancy took the brush from her backpack. It was the type of brush that rockhounds and archaeologists used to brush off specimens. As she ran her fingers across the soft hairs, she felt a tingle of recognition. She took the golden brown camel hairs she had found on the professor's windowsill and compared them with a couple of hairs from Lia's brush. Under the microscope, the hairs looked exactly the same.

"What are you thinking?" Ned asked.

"Remember, the phone message said that the professor threatened the blackmailer and now he had to make the final payment. The blackmailer and the poisoner must be the same person. Ever since we've been involved in the case, the incidents have escalated. It's as if someone's trying to sabotage the camp, close it down."

Nancy looked at the camel hairs. "I'm sure the police lab will want to run more thorough tests on these hairs," Nancy said. "But if the hairs on the windowsill came from Lia's brush—"

"Are you thinking it's Lia?" Ned asked. "That Lia poisoned Professor Parris?"

"The professor said he met with her the night before he collapsed; they were working out the quarry field trip. The amanitin can take up to forty-eight hours for symptoms to appear."

"That gives her opportunity," Ned commented.

"She sure has expert knowledge of poisons. And the poison seems to be some sort of special recipe—other things added to the Death Angel mushroom extract. She says her lab is trying to find an antidote. She's an adviser to the Rocks, yet she didn't go on the field trip. She had a good excuse by meeting with the doctors at the hospital at that time, so it didn't seem suspicious then. But she could have arranged it that way—*after* setting the trap in that stone pyramid."

"She could sure do that," Ned said. "The quarry's definitely her turf."

"My turf, yes," said a lilting voice from behind them. "And now it will become your tomb."

15

The Leader Returns

Nancy turned slowly, knowing what she would find. When she faced the door, she felt her knees buckle a little, and she leaned back against the cupboard. She could hear Ned breathing rapidly beside her. Neither spoke as they looked at the figure standing inside the doorway.

The light was a little dim at that end of the lab, but Nancy could see a person dressed in navy blue slacks and sweater. A gas mask hung from one belt loop, a rope from another. The person's left hand held a glass jar. A ski mask covered most of the face, but there was no mistaking the voice or those blazing black eyes.

"Lia," Nancy said, her voice nearly a whisper.

"I have been listening to you for a few minutes," Lia said. "Your reputation as an accomplished detective is well earned, it seems."

"Now, look," Ned said, leaning forward. "There're two of us and only one of you—"

"You're mistaken," Lia said. "I have a powerful ally here." She held up the jar. "Hydrosulfuric acid. I followed you here from the restaurant and have come prepared. I assure you that if you breathe the vapor trapped in this jar, your reaction will be immediate and very unpleasant. Do not test me on this."

Nancy remembered from her high school chemistry class that the vapor known as hydrogen sulfide was a powerful gas that could cause death within thirty minutes. "We believe you," Nancy told Lia. She felt Ned lean back into the cupboard.

"So you were blackmailing Professor Parris," Nancy said.

"That's right, I was," Lia answered. "I have friends and colleagues all over the world. A couple of them in Australia helped me put together the pieces to confirm that Charles used to be Shep Jackson, a man once tried for murder."

"He was just charged, never tried," Ned said.

"Nevertheless, not something a man like Charles wants known," Lia said. "My plan was simple enough at first. "I'd do it anonymously—no one would ever know. I needed money, and this seemed like an easy way to get it. I knew Charles could afford it. After all, he's a worldwide celebrity in forensics," she added with a sneer.

"You seem jealous of him," Nancy said.

"Why shouldn't I be?" Lia said, her voice tight. "I worked as hard as he did. I also developed new methods and new techniques. But Charles—*an accused murderer*—gets the glory, and the income that comes with it."

"Your simple plan seemed to have worked for a while," Nancy said. "But something must have gone wrong, or you'd still be collecting money. What happened?"

"He agreed at first to my demands in order to guarantee my silence. He didn't know that I was the one contacting him, of course. But then he started making noises about finding out who was blackmailing him and threatening to call the FBI. I knew then I had to silence him. If anyone found out I'd been blackmailing him, I'd be ruined."

"So you poisoned him," Nancy said.

"That's right," Lia said. "With my own custom recipe." Her dark eyes crinkled around the corners. Nancy was shocked to realize that the woman was probably smiling beneath the ski mask.

"Did you administer the poison Friday evening, while you met about the quarry trip?" Nancy asked.

"That's right," Lia said. "It was very easy. I was

sure the camp would be canceled after his collapse. But then I learned that you were going to be in charge, and I was afraid you might come across some evidence of the blackmail."

"So you decided to break into the office Sunday night," Nancy said.

"Yes—and there you were," Lia said. "In my way!"

"So you're the one who clobbered Nancy in the parking lot," Ned said.

"But still you wouldn't get off the case." Lia started pacing, swinging the jar.

Nancy kept her ears open, but her eyes on the jar. She reached back and eased the cupboard door open. She slid her hand inside. Slowly, quietly, she felt around the shelf until she found what she wanted. It was the pint jar of limestone dust that the Rocks had accumulated when they sliced the quarry specimens. Carefully she worked her fingers and thumb around the lid and began unscrewing it.

"And you're the one who released the chlorine gas that knocked out Bess and Mimi?" Nancy asked. She had to keep Lia distracted, keep her talking until she could get the lid off.

"Yes," Lia answered. "I decided to make things so dangerous around here that the camp would shut down altogether. I released the chlorine gas here in the lab. And I set the trap at the quarry. It would have been better if one of the campers had fallen in and gotten hurt. The camp surely would have been closed down then."

"But it was George," Ned said.

"Yes," Lia said, with a disappointed tone. "I knew that if I could just get all the campers and real investigators and amateur detectives out of here, I could concentrate on my real goal—making sure Charles never spoke again."

"Oh, no," Nancy said. "I just realized. You've been sabotaging the experimental antidotes." She felt a shudder of horror down her spine as she spoke, then a thrill of hope as she lifted the lid off the pint of rock grit in the cupboard.

"Of course," Lia said. "You don't think I'd ruin my own superior poison recipe." She took the rope from her belt. "Well, I'm tired of taking such small measures and getting such meaningless results. I must get you off the case. If I can't scare you off, I'll just have to take you off permanently."

She walked slowly toward Nancy and Ned. "Now we'll go for our ride to the quarry. Ned, you'll drive. But first, take this rope and tie up your friend here. And don't fake it. I'll be checking carefully."

Nancy was so focused on Lia coming toward them, on the jar in Lia's hand, and on her own hand on the jar of limestone dust, that she practically stopped breathing. She knew she'd have only one chance.

She waited until the moment Ned had his hands on the rope. Then, with all her strength, she pulled her arm around in a huge swoop. She flung the limestone grit at Lia's face, aiming as best she could for those huge black eyes.

"Ned, grab her!" Nancy yelled, watching the jar in Lia's left hand.

Lia's right hand shot to her face, clawing at the ski mask and swiping at her eyes. She twisted around and made a strange gurgling noise.

Ned jumped at Lia and grabbed her from behind.

The lethal jar swung around, sailing out of Lia's grip. Nancy, her eyes never leaving the jar, plucked it out of the air and drew it to her. She quickly took it to the lab cupboard and shut the door.

Then she returned to help Ned tie up Lia with her own rope.

Hill responded to Nancy's call almost immediately. Nancy told him what had happened.

"You should have seen her catch that jar," Ned said proudly. "She's ready for the Super Bowl!"

"Great job, Nancy," Hill said, while a police officer took Lia and the jar of hydrosulfuric acid away. "What made you suspect her anyway?"

Nancy told Hill about checking the camel hairs from the windowsill against Lia's brush, and repeated what Lia had told them during her attack.

While Nancy talked, Ned called Christy and told her what had happened.

"So what do you want to do about camp?" Hill asked. He reached into his duffel bag and pulled out a roll of bright yellow tape, the kind used by police to rope off a crime scene to protect evidence.

"It looks like the lab's going to be off limits," Nancy said as Hill unrolled the tape.

"I'm afraid so," Hill said. "I'll have my crew start gathering evidence right away, but I don't know how long it will take. I can't have the campers trudging through the lab until we know we have everything we need."

"Christy was stunned by Lia's arrest," Ned said, returning from his phone call. "She wants to know if we're going to close the camp."

"That's just what we were talking about," Nancy said. "And I have an idea. We could use this case— the real mystery and crimes—as a practical workshop in forensic science."

"What do you have in mind?" Hill asked.

"The teams wrapped up their testing today, anyway," Nancy pointed out. "They're scheduled to finish their analysis and reports tomorrow morning. In the afternoon the district attorney and a judge were scheduled to talk to them about evidence and court procedure."

"Then Friday is the Solution Breakfast," Ned added. "That's when the teams present their solutions to the camp crime."

"Let's change the schedule a little," Nancy suggested. "They'll still finish their reports tomorrow morning. The campers take their notes home each afternoon, so they don't need to come to the lab. We can meet in the library while they prepare their reports. Then we'll have a Solution Lunch and meet with the DA and judge as scheduled."

"So the campers reveal their culprits tomorrow?" Ned asked. "But what about Friday?"

"Friday we'll spend the whole day on the *real* crimes," Nancy said. "It's all going to be in the newspaper anyway. The campers will feel cheated if we don't at least talk about it."

"Do we tell them everything?" Ned asked.

"Everything," Nancy said. "The professor's poisoning, how the chlorine gas was no accident, why George disappeared at the quarry—all of it. Of course, we'll be careful to protect Lia's rights. We don't want to jeopardize the trial."

"The campers will love it," Hill said.

"Good," Nancy said. "I'll tell the counselors." Nancy and Ned headed off to their homes, leaving Hill to secure the lab. When Nancy got home, the first thing she did was call Bess and George to fill them in. Then she checked in with Christy.

"Nancy, it's a great idea," Christy said when Nancy told her the plan. "Uncle Charles will love it, too. Using a fictional crime is good, but using the real crimes will be great. That will *really* show the campers how to use science to solve crimes!"

"Okay," Nancy said. "We'll announce the change tomorrow morning. See you then."

Nancy spent a few moments in bed jotting notes for the next day but fell asleep with the pencil still in her hand.

Thursday morning Nancy and the other counselors were waiting on the shuttle for the campers. During the ride to the library, Nancy announced the change of schedule.

"Cool," Antoine said. The other campers nodded their agreement.

"Wow, real crimes," Janie Silver Cloud murmured. "And all happening right here in camp!"

When they got to the library, the four teams immediately went to work in one of the conference rooms, wrapping up their reports.

Hill arrived at eleven o'clock and pulled Nancy and the counselors aside. "I have wonderful news," he said. "Lia finally gave us her poison recipe, so now the doctors are administering the right antidotes to Charles. They expect a long recovery period, but the prognosis is good. He's even regained consciousness."

"Oh, I can't believe it," Christy said. "Is he talking?"

"He is," Hill answered. "He admitted to being Shep Jackson but swears he never murdered anyone. I believe him. When he was still in high school, he had a big falling-out with his stepfather and ran away. He chose Australia because his birth father lived there. He looked him up, took back his old name, and lived with his birth father for a few years until he died. Then Charles started college there in Sydney."

"That's when he was arrested," Nancy said.

"Yes," Hill said. "He's spent most of his life since then trying to put together proof of his innocence, so he could clear his name."

"Even though it was so long ago and so far away?" Ned asked. "And there never was a trial?"

"He's a very proud man, and he can't stand to have this cloud over his head," Hill said. "The mysterious empty envelope with the Australian stamp contained some of the evidence, which he removed and kept in a safe in his house."

"It must have been awful to be blackmailed," Bess said, "after keeping his secret so long."

"And he went to so much trouble," Hill pointed out. "All those notes in his journal—'meeting with S. Jackson,' 'must keep SJ quiet,' 'can't let SJ resurface.'"

"Yeah, what was all that?" George asked.

146

"Just notes to himself about leads he was following," Hill answered. "He said he wrote them in a sort of code so that if the journal was found, no one would think *he* was Jackson or SJ."

"And it worked," Nancy said, "for a while."

At noon everyone gathered at the cafeteria for the Solution Lunch. Nancy heard a buzz of excitement around the room as she ate. Finally it was time to reveal the culprits. Each team talked about the evidence, and each was guided by its unique clue to a different solution.

"Our special clue was the torn piece of cloth caught in the window," the Rags team representative, Dee Haze, announced. "We matched it to a blouse owned by the wife, so she did it."

Isaiah explained the procedures used by the Rocks team. "The gravel at the crime scene came from the lake cottage owned by the victim's business partner, so he did it," he concluded.

Mimi revealed that the hairs in the carpet were dog hairs, as she explained the solution arrived at by the Locks. "The victim's neighbor has a dog with the same hair. He did it."

"Well, our culprit was the craziest," Mario announced, speaking for the Chomps. "It was the victim himself. He faked his own death, planting a tooth at the scene of the crime. But the tooth wasn't knocked out during the murder. It was one he'd lost a long time ago—and saved!"

After all the presentations concluded, Hill told the campers about the professor's recovery. "The antidote is doing its job, and thanks to Nancy and her team, he will be able to concoct another camp crime scenario for next year." The cafeteria exploded in a rousing cheer.

"Well, of course, I'm not surprised she figured it all out," Bess added with a grin. "After all, for Nancy Drew, life is just one big Crime Lab Camp!"

American S·I·S·T·E·R·S

Join different sets of sisters as they embark on the varied, sometimes dangerous, always exciting journeys across America's landscape!

West Along the Wagon Road, 1852

A *Titanic* Journey Across the Sea, 1912

Voyage to a Free Land, 1630

Adventure on the Wilderness Road, 1775

Crossing the Colorado Rockies, 1864

Down the Rio Grande, 1829

Horseback on the Boston Post Road, 1704

Exploring the Chicago World's Fair, 1893

Pacific Odyssey to California, 1905

by Laurie Lawlor

Published by Simon & Schuster

Step back in time with Warren and Betsy
through the power of the Instant Commuter invention
and relive, in exciting detail, the greatest
natural disasters of all time...

PEG KEHRET'S

THE VOLCANO DISASTER
Visit the great volcano eruption of Mount St. Helens
in Washington on May 18, 1980. . . .

THE BLIZZARD DISASTER
Try to survive the terrifying blizzard of
November 11, 1940 in Minnesota. . . .
Iowa's Children's Choice Award Master List

THE FLOOD DISASTER
Can they return to the Johnstown Flood
of May 31, 1889 in time to save lives?
Iowa Children's Choice Award Master List
Florida Sunshine State Award Master List

Published by Simon & Schuster

3017-02